Author Note

It's amazing how dreams become so achievable once you remove outside forces from them. I never thought I could publish a book, not to mention two. For many ambitions, you hear how important networking, and platform-building, and publicity is. What a large role it plays in accomplishing what you desire. And while there is truth to that, I will also say:

Before you throw yourself entirely into something, first figure out why you want it.

Do you want people to know who you are? Do you want to be invited to the Oscars, and The Met Gala? Do you like to learn, or practice, or perform? For me, I love the art. I love the feeling when words begin to dance across my screen before I even have the chance to decide if I want them. I love giving real representation to those who feel ignored in literature. And once I realized that, it only took me six months to reach my lifelong goal of becoming a published author.

No, I didn't build a giant following on social media. Nor did I land an agent or a traditional publishing deal. But none of those things matter, because my goal was to write. And write, I did.

To those of you who have found this novella because you read my novel, Puppy Love, thank you. Well Written wouldn't be possible without the love, and support you guys have given me. Writing is a beautiful thing, and it's one of my favorite activities, but publishing is hard, and it's the dedicated readers that help the motivation continue.

Now, before you turn the page to immerse yourself into this story, there are a few things you must know. Firstly, this book is a novella. If you don't know what that means, it's like my dogs' attention spans: Short. Novellas are intended to be more brief, and fast-paced. So if you're looking for a 350 page slow-burn, realistic romance, well, Puppy Love may be more suited for you. This is a binge-read. A palate-refresher. As Sabrina Carpenter would say, it's short and sweet. That being said, please read below for some very important trigger warnings. Your health is of the upmost importance to me, so take them into careful consideration.

Trigger Warnings: homophobia (internal and external), graphic depictions of sex, severe depression, alcohol consumption, SSRI medication, and suicidal ideation.

Again, if any of these topics are triggering or unhealthy for you to consume, please proceed with extreme caution, or select another book to safely satisfy your needs. For those who wish to continue, another important note:

This book contains a character who has severe, clinical depression. As with most illnesses, physical and mental, this disease affects people in many different ways. I wrote this character in a way I knew to be true, from both personal experience, and thorough research. I truly

Well Written

SOME LOVE STORIES DESERVE A SECOND DRAFT.

ELLE SPRINKLE

hope those who struggle with the illness as well feel as though this was produced tastefully, and with care.

If you or a loved one are struggling with suicidal ideation, please reach out to a loved one, or call your local suicide hotline. I know it's hard to believe there is light at the end of the tunnel, but if you feel as if nobody cares, know that I always do.

Thank you to everyone reading this, for your decision to pick up my book, and help my dream come true. I can't wait to introduce you to my lovely men, Kane Ramirez and Marcus Fraund.

xoxo,

Elle

To the ones who feel like they'll never get better.
I know that it's hard. It probably always will be. But hold onto those rare, fleeting moments of light, for as long as you remember them, they will be more powerful than your years of sadness.

Prologue

CLARA

Friday 4:56PM

From: wellwrittenbooks@wellwrittenbooks.com
To: jrosebarlowe@carsenvlovett.com
Subject: The Thread Untied Book Tour

Janelle,

Hello! I know you are a very busy woman, and I sincerely appreciate you taking time out of your day to read this email. This is a bit unorthodox, but I heard some talk from my friend Barry— he's a publisher—- do you know him? Anyway, he mentioned that there was talk about Mr. Lovett doing a book tour for his new release, *The Thread Untied*. Things don't usually work this way, I know, but I wondered if there was any possibility of him making a stop at our store. It's the cutest little shop in Coral Beach Oregon, the views are *amazing.*

You see, my ex-husband (long story) co-owns the store with me, and is going through a rough time. Mr. Lovett has been his favorite author since the first book he published. Like, seriously, he's *obsessed.* It would make his day, hell, his *life* if Carsen added Well Written to his tour. I know sometimes these things are out of your hands, but what's that saying? "The answer is always 'no' if you never ask?" I don't know, something like that.

Anyway, let me know!
Clara
Well Written Books
www.wellwrittenbooks.com
3851 E Sunset Ave, Coral Beach, Oregon

Monday 9:37AM

Sender: jrosebarlowe@carsenvlovett.com
To: wellwrittenbooks@wellwrittenbooks.com
Re: The Thread Untied Book Tour

Clara,

I have to say, your email was a delightful find amongst piles and piles of spam. And *junk*, if you catch my drift.

I spoke with Mr.Lovett about your request, and he was absolutely *ecstatic* to hear from your store. He mentioned that he had been there years ago, and has very fond memories of the place. So fond, in fact, that he wanted me to see if the invitation could be extended into a full launch-party. We are more than happy to cover any expenses this may incur.

Hope to hear from you soon,
Janelle Barlowe
Assistant to Carsen V. Lovett

Monday 9:38AM

Sender: wellwrittenbooks@wellwrittenbooks.com
To: jrosebarlowe@carsenvlovett.com
Re:The Thread Untied Book Tour

Janelle,
Hell. Yes.

Clara
Well Written Books
www.wellwrittenbooks.com
3851 E Sunset Ave, Coral Beach, Oregon

Chapter One

KANE

Summers in Oregon remind me a lot of my ex-wife Clara, in the way that they're unpredictable. One minute, the sun is beaming through the arched windows of Well Written Books. The next, the thin panes rattle against the frame as thick drops of rain pound against them, heavy thunder sending vibrations through the shelves. I don't mind the versatility of it. I just wish it was more calculable.

I don't like surprises.

Birthday parties, puppies in boxes, proposal flash mobs. It's all a bit much, don't you think? Clara says that I'm just no fun. When I asked her to marry me all those years ago, she knew it was coming. Not because I suggested she get her nails done or because she found the sapphire ring tucked away in the bottom of the sock drawer, but because I had told her I was going to ask. And when, and how.

I wasn't trying to ruin the surprise, I was trying to *erase* it. I mean, if you're planning to spend the rest of your life with someone, it probably shouldn't come as a shock to them. Clara sees it differently.

She thinks surprises are fun, and romantic. Spontaneous bouts of affection that prove love is unpredictably magnificent. That's why she returned that little blue ring two years ago, and replaced it with a thick-cut diamond. It's also why she's yelling at me right now, in the middle of the bookstore we still own together.

"You're being *ridiculous*," she yells, waving around a paperback copy of The Great Gatsby. "It's Carsen V. Lovett, not William fucking Shakespeare. He doesn't care if the historical fiction is next to the historical romance."

Her brows pinch together, the corners of her thin pink lips turning down. Clara was always beautiful, but somehow, as she's aged, she's only gotten more so. She tucks a tendril of blonde hair behind her ear, inviting grey strands blending it all together. I take the book from her hand, smoothing out the cover.

"You're bending it," I mutter. I lift the book up, inspecting it closely for any small scratches or nicks. Clara loves books in the way children love their toys. *Roughly*. It's the only thing I hold against her. Despite the divorce, she's still my business partner, and also, my best friend. Strangely enough, her new husband Derrick has quickly made second place.

I set the book back down, adjusting the display by just a hair, so that it's uniform with the others. Clara sighs.

"Kane, I thought you'd be... *excited*. We've had bigger authors than Lovett do signings, and you hardly even *dusted* the place. Why are you taking this so seriously?"

I take off my reading glasses, wiping the smudged lenses carefully with my shirt.

"I *am* excited," I say calmly, though with slight defense. "It's just— I really want him to like it here." I tuck my glasses onto the collar of my shirt.

Carsen V. Lovett. The man is a romance *genius.* Okay, sure, I might not be the best judge of romance myself, but Carsen knows what the hell he's writing about. Contemporary romance is formulaic, but he knows exactly how to be predictable in a way you wouldn't expect. How to create tension out of thin, tangled air. His newest book, *The Thread Untied*, comes out tomorrow, and guess who happens to be hosting the release party?

Clara arranged the entire thing, unbeknownst to me. I can't say I'm angry that she's bringing me face-to-face with my favorite author, but I will admit that the thought makes it feel as though there's water in my lungs. Clara rolls her eyes, but an apologetic smile tugs at the corners of her lips.

"Alright, alright," she puts her hands up, her eyes falling back onto *The Great Gatsby*. She tilts the display back the way it was, then wipes her hands down the front of her jeans. "On your knees for Carsen V. Lovett. Got it."

My eyes roll, but I can't fight the smile forcing its way across my lips. I don't know Carsen V. Lovett, but I can tell you with absolute certainty, judging by the way he writes, I *would* get on my knees for him.

"Oh fuck off Clara. Don't you have a diaper to change?"

Clara and Derrick recently had a baby. A boy, named Judah Kane Williams. Most people would find it strange that their ex-wife and her new husband named their child after them, but like I said, they're my *best friends.* Plus, Kane is a pretty sweet name. Clara's brows knit together, her arms crossing over her chest.

"You know, that sounded really misogynistic," she says. Her gaze falls to my shoulder, the crease in her brow deepening. She licks the pad of her thumb, and begins to rub it against my shirt.

"Stop," I groan, rolling my shoulders back. Her brow twitches.

"You have..." Her eyes narrow in disgust. "What is that? Coffee?"

"It's chocolate, actually," I say proudly, like there's anything to be proud of. "From the croissant I got from La Luna Cafe this morning."

"That's been there since this morning?" she asks, a seemingly irritated stream of air flowing from her pursed lips. "You *seriously* need to shower, Kane. The locals might recognize you, but the tourists are going to think you're *living* in here."

Rude, though she's not entirely wrong. The economy in Coral Beach Oregon almost exclusively thrives off the tourists. Tourists that admittedly, lately, have been looking at me like I'm a stray, flea-ridden cat. It's not like I don't take care of myself. I shower, most days, and I always make sure I smell nice. It's just hard to keep up with the rest of it when I have so many other things on my mind. Yeah, maybe my mustache is going a little rogue. So what?

"I shower," I grumble, pushing her hand off the stain on my shirt. Clara rolls her eyes dramatically, then checks her watch. "You're not driving in this weather."

She shakes her head, pulling out her phone. "Derrick's picking me up. I was hoping to be here when your *celebrity crush* arrived—" I grunt, but she ignores me. "—but I really can't miss Judah's checkup. Are you going to be okay without me, or should I send a babysitter so you don't jump his bones?"

The corners of her lips pull into a teasing smirk, and I suck in my cheeks to hide my amusement. Clara wins at everything. Bingo, giveaways, comebacks, *life.* She doesn't get to win this.

"We're just going over the plan for tomorrow. I think I'll manage," I say. She looks at me sweetly this time, her hand reaching out and grabbing mine. Clara's skin is so soft, and gentle. Her eyes are warm and intelligent. She's the whole package, and still, she just wasn't the one for me. Sometimes when I look at her, I wonder if there even is a "one". Because if someone so smart, and beautiful, so caring and stubborn as Clara didn't work out, then who will?

"Alright," she says, and quite softly. "Are you okay, Kane?"

My brows knit together, my head tilting in confusion.

"What do you mean?"

Clara shakes her head, her hand squeezing mine. "I'm just checking," she says gently. "You seem a bit... *down* is all."

I chew the inside of my cheek as I swallow, marinating in her words for just a moment too long.

"You can talk to me, Kane. And Derrick too. You're family, you know?"

I nod, forcing a smile that I hope she doesn't see through.

"Yes, I know. Thank you, Clara. But I'm fine."

By the concerned glaze over her eyes, I can tell she's unconvinced. But just as her lips part to speak, her phone rings. She releases my hand, and lifts it to her ear.

"Hello? Okay, alright babe. I'll be right out." She looks up at me and smiles. "I'll tell him. Okay, I love you too."

When the call ends, she slides her phone carefully into her back pocket.

"Derrick says you two need to go out soon. He needs his 'Kane Time'." She chuckles. A soft laugh slips through my lips and my gaze drifts to the floor as I shuffle my feet.

"Yeah, I suppose we're due for that," I reply. When I look back up, Clara's purse is slung over her shoulder, her hand propped confidently on her hip.

"Seriously, Kane," she says again. "Talk to us. Come over for dinner, get out of the house. You need to—" She pauses, looking me up and down. "—*do* something."

This isn't a new conversation for us. Actually, its a decades old argument. And its the reason she helped me buy Well Written Books in the first place: to get me out of the house. It helped, along with the Doxepin. But lately, it just hasn't been as effective as it used to be. Neither of them are.

"*Okay,*" I answer agitatedly, though I know Clara's just pushing because she cares. That's her thing. Annoying you with her *unconditional* love. "Tomorrow night? After the signing?"

Clara nods in approval, then spins around on her toes, walking toward the exit. Rain patters against the sidewalk, the sound flooding my eardrums as she opens the door. She looks over her shoulder, smacking her palm against her forehead.

"I totally forgot," she groans, wiping the hand down her face. "I got locked out of the email somehow. Can you take a look at it please?"

My brows furrow, confused. Clara is much more adept at solving technological issues than I am. But if she wants me to handle it, I will try my absolute hardest for her.

"Sure," I nod, and she smiles at me appreciatively.

"Love you, Sugar Kane!" she calls out, and the door slams closed behind her.

From the stock room, I hear little clawed feet tapping against the old hardwood. I turn around, patting my thigh softly to beckon Dickie to my side.

Dickinson is the French Bulldog that Clara rescued for me soon after our divorce. She worried about me being alone, not that I ever *could* be alone with friends as clingy as her and Derrick. Back when his name was Poe, his owner passed away from cancer. The family didn't know what to do with him, so they surrendered him to the shelter. Or maybe that's just what Clara said so that I felt guilty enough to take him in. Anyway, "Poe" was a little too dark and mysterious for a dog of his candid lovingness, so I changed it to Dickinson.

Dickie lets out a snort reminiscent to a pig, pawing at me with his front foot. I sigh, leaning down and scooping him up.

"You're a spoiled brat," I mumble, but I smile as he presses his wet nose against my ear. I have to admit that while annoying, Dickie has made the whole "alone" of it all much easier. Even on days I struggle to pull myself from my gritty bed sheets, he's there, forcing me to try so that he can go outside, and wander the world.

Having depression is like playing Russian Roulette, at least for me. It hits differently each day. Sometimes, I can't get out of bed at all. I just lay there, from dawn until dusk, staring at the ceiling while each piece of me rots away. My body sweats, my brain decomposing into nothing but fragments of pity and self-loathing. Other days, I can't stay in bed at all. I walk down moonlit streets wondering why the pit in my stomach is undefeatable, why I can be surrounded by love and support and opportunity, and be so selfishly unhappy.

Not to say I'm ungrateful for the world around me, or for the people in it. I try my hardest not to take it all for granted. When I step outside, I close my eyes and breathe in the salty ocean air. I soak in every minute with Clara and Derrick and Judah, and remind myself to always treasure it like it's the last. I take Dickie on walks along the coast, letting him stop to sniff every broken shell and piece of driftwood that washes to shore.

That's what so frustrating.

I cherish the small things. I take my meds, and I try not to wallow when I have the energy to do anything else. I do *everything* I'm supposed to, and still, I feel this way. I always have.

I carry Dickie over to the stained glass window against the front wall, setting him on top of the cushioned bench before turning to the shelves and reaching for my comfort book. Really, it shouldn't be comforting at all.

Harrison's Affair by Carsen V. Lovett is a pretty heartbreaking novel, up until the end. It's what you'd call an "angsty" slow-burn romance, the characters constantly fighting and pulling apart throughout the majority of the book. Still I can't help but admire the validity of it, the relatability. Sometimes, though, it feels a bit too reminiscent of my own relationship.

Not with Clara, of course. That relationship probably holds a historical record for being exceptionally uneventful. But the one before that, my lover from college. Sometimes, it feels like *Harrison's Affair* was based off of it. The sad main character, the closeted love interest. It's like someone experienced the excruciating love that I did, and made it out alive to tell the story. The worst part is, Carsen V. Lovett did a really good job. He perfectly captured the torture it is to love someone who hates the part of them that loves you. And what he did even better, was acknowledge that that type of love never really goes away.

You'll always wonder what would have happened if they had simply accepted themselves. You'll always want to know if they were the only person who could ever really love you, because you both were equally and perpetually sad. You'll always think about what life would be like if the world wasn't so cruel and hating.

I settle into the bench, my hip pressed to the window and my back against a bookshelf. Dickie crawls onto my lap as I crack the hardcover open, the old wooden window nook creaking unsteadily beneath us as he moves. Taking the mechanical pencil hooked to the collar of my shirt, I begin to scribble notes into the margins of the pages as I read.

I've read this book countless times, but I only started annotating it a few weeks ago. It helps, I think.

I love the way the graphite sounds against the smooth, cream-colored pages. I love how so many of the ineligible scribbles are meaningless to everyone but me. I love that the person who wrote the original text understands me in a way nobody else seems to.

Like most things in life, it's bittersweet. The beautiful imagery, and wholehearted paragraphs, remind me that I haven't felt understood by a person in nearly twenty years.

When the storm clouds roll in

And droplets begin to fall

I will take your hand

Pull you off the worn-seated bench

And dance with you in the rain

-MF

Chapter Two

MARCUS

My hand wraps around a white t-shirt, tossing it across the room at the half-naked man whose name I've already forgotten.

"Thanks," he grins, pulling it over his head. He tugs it down over his torso, each rib in his body prominently peeking from beneath the skin. I nod.

"Sure."

I look down at my pants as I button them. Why do I feel like the buttons on slacks are always too big for the hole? Fumbling around with it, it feels as if a pair of eyes are burning through the top of my skull. My gaze flicks back to the man.

"What?" I ask, my brow lifted slightly. The man stares back at me, his emerald green eyes scanning mine like I hold the answer to my own question. He clears his throat.

"I was just wondering if you wanted to get some lunch," he says, sliding a pair of aviators onto the v-necked collar of his shirt.

Look, this guy was fun, I'll admit that. But that's exactly the point. The fun stops the second things go further than casual sex in a mediocre coastal hotel room. I look down at my sleeves, folding the cuffs backward messily.

"I can't," I say, and it feels good to know that it isn't a lie. *This time.* "I have a meeting."

The man nods, and I sense a slight disappointment in the movement, but he simply shrugs.

"Cool," he says, reaching for his jacket hanging over the chair. "See you around, then."

My forehead tightens when I lift my brows, and I watch as he walks out of the room swiftly, the door closing behind him. I let out a breath.

Something about kicking out hookups is particularly stressful, which is why I'm always straightforward with people in the beginning. I don't want them to think there's any part of me that's looking for more. Still, sometimes, they try anyway. I guess "visiting my hometown for a weekend while on a tour for my new book" could also be perceived as "convince me to stay." Or at least that guy seemed to think so.

Walking into the lowly-lit bathroom, I glance into the mirror, my grey hair a messy display of the activity that just transpired. I dig through my toiletry bag, grabbing a comb and slicking it back tediously. Then, my thumb tucks in between the soft layers of my shirt, popping the top button open. If I remember anything about Coral Beach, it's that it isn't a "fully buttoned" kind of town. Tucked away on the Oregon Coast, its a quaint, but popular city. And though I moved on nearly twenty years ago, I can't say that I hate being back.

Some things are still the same. The salty ocean breeze, the sudden weather fluctuation, The Seahorse Inn, apparently. But not everything can remain untouched.

The roads are new. Dark, leveled asphalt superseding the previous ashy, jagged gravel. With the extinction of the dusty clouds the tires' friction once created, the view to my childhood home was clear as we drove to the hotel yesterday. Like the renewed streets, that too, has changed. The once tiny beach bungalow now stands two stories tall, a balcony fit for kings enveloping its entirety.

I wondered briefly who lives there. If the ghosts of my younger years haunt the walls the way they used to haunt me. But the pristine slotted shutters were enough to confirm that those ghosts are long forgotten. I guess as far as changes go, that one is definitely for the better.

Well Written Books, on the other hand, I cannot attest. The idea that *anyone* could love that place the way Old Man Duke did proves to be unfathomable. Still, with his passing in recent years, it's only fair that I pay tribute to the place that created me. And what better way to pay tribute, than to have Well Written Books host the launch party for my newest release, *The Thread Untied?*

In college, the bookstore was practically my haven. It didn't pay well, but I didn't care. The wealth to me lied in the pages on the shelves, and with the people I met inside. In fact, I met my first lover while working at Well Written Books. Actually, my *only* lover.

An incessant rapping erupts from my hotel door, a recognizable, and rather annoyed voice heightening behind it.

"Marcus?" Janelle announces, loud enough for the entire hall to hear. "Your driver is supposed to be here in two minutes!"

I check the time on my phone, a bright *1:38* shining up at me through the screen.

"Shit!"

I rush out of the bathroom, looking around until I locate my jacket. Peeking at my hair in the mirror one last time, I shake it around to make it just less than perfect, before quickly opening the door to greet Janelle.

"Sorry," I say, sliding my arms through the sleeves of my sweatshirt. Nellie glances at the unmade bed behind me, cocking a sculpted dark brow as her eyes meet mine. I let an awkward, apologetic smile creep across my face.

"Really?" she huffs. I shrug.

"I had some time to kill."

"You always 'have time to kill', even when you actually *don't*."

Nellie is rather bossy for an assistant, but that's exactly why I hired her. I need someone direct enough to keep track of me, to make sure I'm meeting my deadlines and showing up on time. She's intolerant to tardiness, and made that clear in the beginning when I was three minutes late to her interview.

"I should have left," she said shortly, impatiently tapping the tip of her pen against the table. "Tell me why I didn't."

While I was shocked that she would start her interview like that, it impressed me. Janelle knew her worth, and I needed an assistant who understood mine as well.

"Sorry," I said breathily, sitting in the seat across from her. "Traffic." That was a total lie, and Janelle knew it. Still, she didn't budge.

"Tell me why I didn't leave," she says again, straightening her posture. My brows furrowed, and I tilted my head.

"You're...serious?"

Janelle's arms crossed over her chest. "I'm still sitting here, aren't I?"

Humored by her demands, I decided to indulge. My gaze traveled down her body, settling onto her hands. A lustrous grey residue painted along the side of her left-hand pointer finger and thumb.

"You're left-handed," I stated curiously, letting my eyes wander further. Something reflective caught my attention, and my eyes narrowed onto the object. A small, enamel pin lived on the handle of her tote bag, the design inside immediately familiar. Rather than point it out, however, I continued my motionless journey. When my gaze fell onto the iced coffee rested on the table beside her, I knew that I won.

I also knew she wouldn't be happy about it.

"You're a writer," I said evenly, holding back the triumph in my voice. Janelle's perfect brows weaved together, and she slumped back in her chair, though I don't think she realized it.

"So your attention to detail goes further than your books," she stated, in a rather surprised tone. "I have to say, as a fan, I'm relieved. But it doesn't apply to your timeliness?"

"That's what I need you for," I answered. "My timeliness."

Publishing is an intense industry, and keeping up with it began to feel unachievable. Every year, I'm demanded a new project, one I don't even get full autonomy over, with a deadline that's nearly impossible to meet. Then I have to follow it up with interviews, and spin-offs, and tours. It was fun, at first. I liked the distraction that was publicity, and it felt good to be known for the person I am instead of the person I was. But as due dates got tighter, I began to find it more and more difficult to do my stories, my characters, the justice they deserved. The hope was that if my time was better managed, my passion would thrive.

Janelle looked me up and down shamelessly, tapping her acrylic nails against the table as if deep in thought. I was supposed to be the one interviewing her, yet at that moment, I felt like I was being fired.

"Columbia is impressive!" I exclaimed somewhat frantically, pointing to the pin shining on her bag. Janelle glanced at it, then looked back up at me, like I was some poor, lost puppy.

Then, she let out an embarrassingly long sigh. "You're going to help me become a published author," she stated firmly. A wave of relief washed over me, and for some reason, it felt like I had just won the lottery. She stood quickly, slinging her bag over her shoulder, and scooping up her half-melted coffee. "And I always get Mondays off."

We've been inseparable ever since.

"Are you sure you don't want me to come with you?" Nellie asks, her trusty planner gripped in her hands like a precious jewel. We stand beneath the overhang, heavy rainfall thundering against the ridged concrete. This is something I did *not* miss about Coral Springs. A black SUV pulls up against the sidewalk, and I look at Janelle before stepping forward.

"I'm sure," I answer. It's been twenty years since I've stepped foot into Well Written Books. It only feels natural to return the way I left.

Alone.

The tinted passenger window rolls down, the driver inside the car leaning toward it.

"Marcus?" he calls out, his voice nearly consumed by the rain. I nod, then make a break for it, quickly sprinting through the falling droplets into the back seat. "It's really coming down, isn't it?"

I smile.

"Yup. Not quite like Phoenix," I say back. The driver raises a brow, his eyes catching mine through the rear view mirror.

"Phoenix?" he grunts. "Escaping the heat or somethin'?"

I adjust the cuff of my sleeve again as I maintain eye contact. His irises are reminiscent to the ones I inherited from my mother, a dusty shade of blue that forces me to look away.

"A book tour," I answer. "And this is my hometown."

The driver nods, satisfied with my response, then pulls away from the curb, beginning the short drive to Well Written Books. Like most people I meet, he asks about my writing, and my new release, and my plans for the next one, and when we arrive at the bookstore, I hand him a business card with my information on it before hopping out.

"Thanks Mr..." He looks down at the business card, then back up at me. "*Lovett*. I'll definitely be there tomorrow."

I give him a polite wave as he pulls away, then hastily make my way inside.

There's no telling how much the rain has tousled my hair, but the best thing about Coral Beach is that you're supposed to be a little messy. If you aren't, then you're not living right.

As my body adjusts to the warm comforts of the ancient bookstore, my brain does quite the opposite.

Like the town it lives in, Well Written Books looks just as it did when I left it, yet also, somehow, entirely different. The stained glass window on the wall by the street is as colorful and mesmerizing. Even though the sun is trapped behind thick, dark clouds, the bright gradients make the room glow. Though that could be in part due to the upgraded lighting fixtures, an array of vintage chandeliers dangling from the high ceilings above me. Half of the shelves are new too, deeply stained walnut that brings a strangely classy darkness to the store. I almost love it as much as I once did.

My fingers drag along the books in the romance section, the tips of them dancing over the corner of my debut novel *Harrison's Affair*. It's a well-loved copy, sitting on its own display. The hardcover is worn but clearly cared for. Not a speck of dust lies between the pages, and I flip through it, admiring the admiration. Little handwritten notes are scrawled in the margins in writing so messily passionate that I can't quite make out the words. I tilt my head, adjusting my glasses to get a closer look.

A smile tugs at the corners of my lips as I read:

You still love him, idiot!

I chuckle, continuing to study the penciled annotations.

What a prick.

Been there.

Just move on Harry!

As I try to make out an inarticulate scribble, behind me, someone loudly clears their throat.

"That's actually-" a voice says, the soft waver in it causing all the hairs on the back of my neck to stand. I can't say definitively that it's a voice I've heard before, yet simultaneously, something about it begs to be recognized. "A store copy. You see?"

A thick, taupe finger points to the sign beneath the display, which reads:

DISPLAY COPY ONLY – DO NOT TOUCH

"Sorry," I chuckle, setting the book back onto the acrylic stand. I've been caught before, secretly signing copies I find in airports and bookstores and grocery marts, though I don't think I've ever held one so corrodingly cherished. Regardless, once I inform the employees of my identity, they practically *beg* me to personalize one for them. I plaster on a cheeky smile just before turning around. "Do you want me to sign it?"

My eyes fall down onto a head of fluffy, brown hair. It's greasy, and messy, but that isn't what causes my stomach to sink into the Earth's core. A cowlick sits on the back-left side of his skull, causing the short tufts of hair to sprout in every possible direction. It's adorable, and familiar, and everything in my body pleads for it to belong to someone I haven't yet met.

But over deep brown eyes I've spent my entire adulthood trying to forget, bushy brows shoot up, grazing the hairline of a face I know too well. A face I *knew* too well. A face I've loved.

Just like the first time I met Kane, the air in my lungs freezes. It doesn't flow out, yet I can't breathe in more either. It's like I'm suffocating from my own bodily malfunction.

"Marcus?" Kane asks wearily, blood rushing from his bronzed cheeks. I stay still, my stomach twisting into an immoveable mass.

I should say something. Every alarm bell in my head is pleading desperately for me to do the right thing and speak. But twenty years of silence feels impossible to break. I know I need to say something, but what the fuck is there to say?

How are you?

You remember me?

I'm sorry?

Instead, I repeat myself, like a Russian nesting doll, my voice growing smaller the second time around.

"Do you want me to sign it?" I manage to get out. God, why am I such an idiot?

Kane's richly dark eyes fill briefly with reluctant acceptance, before bewilderment conquers his entire being. His short, broad body stiffens, and the whites of his eyes round out, the color nearly matching that of his cheeks. What could almost be described as a shocked scoff slips from his lips, and he tumbles back into the shelves behind him.

"You're..." He shakes his head, his voice trembling. "*You're* Carsen V. Lovett?"

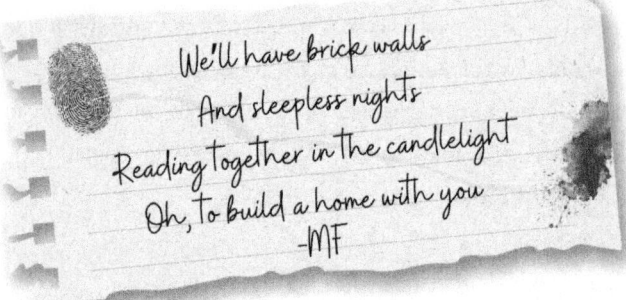

Chapter Three

KANE

If there's anything I've learned from literature, it's that your first love doesn't have to be your greatest. You can fall deeply for someone in your mutual naivety, and fight, and grow, and learn how to be better. How to *love* better. You can move on and find someone who celebrates you, and it isn't any less valuable just because they weren't the first.

But it was different with Marcus.

Clara knew the whole time, but it took me all of seventeen years to realize that Marcus wasn't just the first person I fell in love with. He was the *only* person I fell in love with.

I love Clara with my entire being, and I know she loves me too. But the way her eyes glimmered the first time Derrick walked into the store, it was like I woke up. When the light washed over her as she leaned against the counter, talking and laughing about some joke I didn't understand, it occurred to me that Clara never looked at me the way she had been looking at Derrick. And I couldn't even be upset, because I had never looked at her that way either.

I love Clara with my entire being, but I never fell *in love* with her. I don't know how. Everything about Clara is worthy of love. Her girl-next-door features, how she snorts when she laughs. Her dedication to those she cares for, and how persistent she is in everything she works toward. I think Clara might be the only person on this planet, that has made me feel lovable. She is sweet, and selfless, and proud of me in every way that matters.

She's everything Marcus isn't, and on top of it all, she stayed. So why the hell am I here, twenty years later, staring at him inside of *my* bookstore?

"Kane," he says, though it comes out as a whisper. Marcus is bold, with every fiber of his being. He's a confident man, one who I've always known as a stranger to whispering. With the exception of me, of course. *Us.* We were always a whisper. "What—" His throat clears, and he stands a bit taller. "How have you been?"

His head pulls back slightly, his body towering over me just as it had all those years ago. A grey stubble washes over the sharp, squared jaw that I remember the distinct shape of. One I could identify with my fingertips alone. He looks older, as we all do, but like Clara, he's aged with majesty. Like a painting from another century, more valuable with every passing day.

My heart pounds aggressively, a sharp pinching sensation jolting through my body with each heavy beat. He steps closer, the scent of his cologne bringing a wave of nostalgia with it, years of memories crashing over me in a way that feels cruel. My throat tightens, like a boa constrictor consuming itself. Every second of silence that passes makes me more painfully aware of how close we're standing. How good he smells. How the warmth of his body radiates like a familiar magnet, one I know I need to repel. I step back.

"You're Carsen V. Lovett?" I repeat.

There's no *way* Marcus is Lovett. It's laughable, really. Someone so bitter could never write anything as graceful as Lovett. As devastatingly beautiful. Marcus is the most artificial person I have ever met. He could never write something so *real*. And besides, if Marcus *was* Lovett, I can confidently say that the characters would lack... what's the word... *queerness?*

But when I finally allow my eyes to meet his, no amusement hides behind them. Marcus, for once it seems, is serious. I run my hands through my hair, my gaze falling to the floor as I take a deep, steadying breath.

"A fan?" Marcus asks, his voice nearly teasing.

In another life, I'd play along with him. I'd smile sweetly and tell him to "fuck off". Then I'd push him against the shelves, and press my lips against his. Feel his body melt into mine as if time was a foreign concept. If he never vanished without a word those two decades ago, we'd go home tonight, and he'd read me his latest chapter, asking my opinion on "the flow of the verbiage". We'd kiss goodnight, and maybe I'd feel, for once, like I am not doomed to be miserably alone. Instead, I chew on the inside of my cheek, and try not to think too hard about where it would hurt him most if I were to punch him.

"Hardly," I lie, though maybe I shouldn't. If I tell Marcus the truth, that I've been his biggest fan since his first publication sixteen years ago, his ego might inflate so big he'll pop, and I can spare my knuckles the ache. Marcus chuckles, and this time, when I hear it, I wonder how I didn't recognize it before. There's something so vivacious about it, a record I hate to say I'd play again and again until the vinyl wore thin, each note a pitch that sends goosebumps down my shaggy arms.

"Okay," he says casually. He stands there for a moment, holding a steady, but forced smile on his face, until he quickly breaks, and reaches for my beloved *Harrison's Affair*. "So this *isn't* yours?"

I growl frustratedly, and reach for the book, but he holds it high above my head, just as he did when we were young. His tongue clicks against the roof of his mouth, the previously faux smile transforming into a sly smirk that at least *feels* real. I, however, am not amused. At least something good came from all that heartache, because while I'm sure his devilishly charming looks work on every other human cursed with his presence, I have grown immune.

"*Don't*," I snap between gritted teeth, shocking myself with the coarseness of my tone. Deserved? Probably. But I can't fight the need to follow it up with a much softer "please". That arrogant smile stays glued to his face for a minute, his annoyingly white teeth shimmering in the colorful lights. But as his eyes scan mine, he seems to remember that I, for one, am *always* serious. His smile fades quickly, and he hands the book back to me, clearing his throat.

"I'm sorry. I got carried away. This is all so..." he trails off, and I'd be inclined to believe him, if I knew he possessed the ability to feel remorse. I look down at the book in my hands, running the pad of my index finger along the tarnished foiled letters at the bottom.

Carsen V. Lovett.

I can't believe this is happening.

"Fucked up?" I ask, setting the book back into its resting place on the shelves. Marcus looks at me with furrowed brows, his cheeks sucking in like he's not sure if he's allowed to laugh. "Bizarre? Batshit crazy?"

"I was going to go with 'the world's most discourteous coincidence'," Marcus nods. "But 'batshit crazy' works too."

His eyes lock onto mine, and for some reason, a laugh spills from the both of us. The muscles in my stomach tighten until they ache, and I let the pain simmer for a moment to prove to myself that this is, unfortunately, reality.

What the fuck.

Marcus runs one of his large, pale hands through his perfectly messy hair, the strands flowing back to their natural resting place as he drags his fingers to the back of his neck.

"So." He clears his throat. "What have you been up to?"

The ache in my stomach that was just starting to subside, promptly returns. Though it's fair to assume that this time, it has nothing to do with laughter and contracting muscles. What *have* I been up to? I stand there, silently scraping at another drop of dried chocolate on my jeans I am just now noticing. And it occurs to me, standing face-to-face with the person who broke me, that I will never be able to compete with him, because I haven't done a single damn thing. In the past twenty years, the only thing I've managed to do is *survive.* And what do I have to show for it?

Marcus is successful. He's a renowned, queer author with an extensive backlist, and an even longer catalog of literary awards. He probably lives in a mansion, with an infinity pool and a stupid towel warmer. Like, just use the fucking dryer, you prick. He moved out of this town, and got everything he ever wanted. Meanwhile, I'm here. In the same exact place I was twenty years ago. The same *room*, even. I swallow.

"Did you ever go to Oregon State after graduating Pillar Reef?" he asks. My stomach drops, and that irritating, aching sensation amplifies. After dumping me, Marcus got to live out his dreams. Meanwhile, I was so distraught that I could hardly *breathe.* I didn't go to Oregon State after graduating Pillar Reef University, because I *never graduated* from Pillar Reef. I dropped out during the second quarter of my junior year, and I never went back. But Marcus is already the clear winner of this entire ordeal. I may as well spare myself further embarrassment by bridging the gap just a bit.

"Yeah," I lie, and I hate that my body doesn't believe me. My chest tightens, like it always does when I say "I'm doing better, thanks!" or "Yes, I think the meds are still working." My voice plays the part well enough, though, and Marcus takes the bait. He smiles widely.

"Oh!" His palm claps against my left shoulder blade, and I try not to wince as the skin around it tingles. "I'm so happy to hear that! So how'd you end up at the store? Editing just wasn't doing it for you?"

If Marcus knew the truth, I could say for a fact that he was rubbing giant crystals of salt into my gaping wounds. But of course, he doesn't, so the emotional sting I feel at the mention of editing is entirely karma for lying.

"We should get to it," I deflect, swallowing back the lump in my throat. "I have a lot to do this afternoon."

My gaze falls to the floor, which has always been its natural view. Marcus' shoes are new and pointed. Obviously polished, just like the man himself. I take a moment to look at my own shoes, sandals so worn the straps are nearly disintegrated, dark spots settled where the heel of my foot rests. I wonder what that says about me.

"Okay," he says, his palm dragging against his stubbled cheek. I turn, feeling self conscious for some reason as he follows behind me to the lounging area. Okay, not "for some reason". For *good* reason.

Here he is, showing up after twenty years, in expensive shoes and a successful career, looking like a goddamn sculpture. Meanwhile, I intentionally avoided the mirror this morning, and had no interest in looking for my hairbrush.

As we begin our walk to the back of the store, I hear the familiar *clicking* of Dickies nails behind us. I try to ignore him at first, but Marcus spins around, the soft blue of his eyes deepening as he spots him.

"*You?*" he gasps loudly, a bright smile forcing its way over his face. "*You* have a dog?"

My brows furrow defensively and I lean down, scooping Dickie into my arms.

"I like dogs."

"Sure," he says, his eyebrow cocked in a way that tells me he doesn't believe me. "But you never liked them in the bookstore. You made that *very* clear with Chance."

"*Chance* would always shake water all over the shelves because you *had* to go swimming every lunch break." I roll my eyes, and Marcus shrugs.

"*You* try to keep a retriever out of the water. It's like beaching a whale."

Before I even have the chance to fight it, a smile breaks across my face. I look away quickly, letting my gaze focus onto Dickie for a moment. *Thank god* he's not like Chance.

Chance was a menace to Well Read Books. The fourth summer I worked here, the summer I met Marcus, he'd barrel in through the front door like a bat out of hell, tracking water throughout the store and gnawing on the wooden shelves. Duke used to make Marcus tie him out back under the cedar tree, but Marcus would always sneak him back inside. He was like a little brown velociraptor, Godzilla-ing his way through the bookstore. But Marcus loved that dog with every fiber of his being.

My stomach drops as memories of that summer start to flood my brain, ones I tried hard to forget. I have to admit, though, that every time I walk Dickie along the shore, I can't help but think of the way Chance would follow us around, dragging the biggest piece of driftwood he could find behind him. I hate that still, twenty years later, reminders of that summer take residence in my mind.

"Why are you here, Marcus?" I say finally. The question had been sitting at the very front of my mind since the moment I recognized him. "You spent your entire childhood trying to get out of Coral Beach. You *hated* it here. Why would you come back? Why—" My voice cracks, and I clear my throat. "Why would you come *here?*"

Blood rushes from his cheeks as I spew out the words, the monochrome paleness of his face almost making him appear sick. Like he might pass out. It's so deviant from everything I know about him. From the way he always held himself. I want to feel proud that I gave Marcus just a sliver of the discomfort he gifted me, but the only thing rushing through my veins right now is guilt. Marcus steps closer, his gaze drawing up from Dickie, to me.

"Look, Kane," he says softly. I try to fight it, but my eyes are curious to find what lies inside his. They lock onto the swirling blue irises, and the muscles in my chest tighten uncomfortably. "I will leave, if that's what you truly want. I'll go back to the hotel, pack my things, and catch the first flight out of Portland. I'll refund the party tickets myself, and pay any other expenses involved. Just say the word, and we can pretend I was never here."

My stomach flips as he speaks. I want nothing more than to tell him to go, and to never look back. To never even *think* about letting my name leave his mouth again. But when I try to force the words, I realize that it's a lie. I don't understand it. Twenty years ago, I would've given anything to see Marcus again. But now that he's here, I don't know what I could ever want from him. His apologies are meaningless, as are most things that come from his mouth. Yet, for some reason, even after all this time, I still find myself craving one anyway.

But if that was enough to ask Marcus to stay on its own, I wouldn't be having this internal discourse.

"We have seventy RSVP's," I say, turning away. "Business has been slow. I can't lose the publicity."

Marcus nods understandingly, though his silence sends a wave of malaise through my body. For some, unidentifiable reason, I want to reassure him of my original intentions. Maybe its guilt, or maybe its because the man in front of me has been my secret pleasure and inspiration for years. Whatever it is, I want him to know that Clara didn't agree to hosting the launch for publicity. She did it for *me*.

Oh god. *Clara*. What the *fuck* am I supposed to tell Clara?

"I understand," Marcus says. He straightens his posture, tilts his chin up slightly, and it's crazy how when he holds himself this way, my brain can fill in a crystal clear image of him at twenty-two. "You're right then. We should get to it."

Chapter Four

MARCUS

"I need you to cancel my call with Simeon," I say to Janelle, promptly after stepping out of my ride. She cocks a brow, but immediately pulls her work phone from her back pocket, taps the screen, and presses it to her ear.

"Hi Simeon," she greets sweetly. Nellie has this innate ability to transform into the most angelic, wholesome persona when making business calls. It comes in handy when she has to repeatedly break inconvenient news to people, like letting my agent know that I am, once again, cancelling our meeting. "No, Marcus isn't going to be able to make it again today."

Her pretty brown eyes glance up at me, and a smile that only I know is fake sweeps over her soft, brown cheeks. "Yeah, unfortunately that isn't going to work. He's incredibly sick right now. We might have to cancel the party tomorrow, but I've got some Pedialyte and Tylenol, and am making him rest. Okay, I'll let him know. You too, Simeon." She hangs up, sliding the phone back into her pocket. "God, he's annoying. Do you know how many times I've had to make that call this month?"

Her right hand props against her hip, and her eyes narrow at me disapprovingly.

"You can't avoid him forever, Marc. Either tell him the project isn't working out for you, or figure out how to make it work. But if I have to call him to postpone one more time, I'm quitting."

I quirk a skeptical brow at her, and she rolls her eyes defeatedly.

"Okay, fine, I'm not quitting. But I will Facetime him, and tie you to a chair." She takes my coat off as we step inside the hotel lobby, draping it over her arm.

"What did he want you to tell me?" I ask, rubbing my temples with my fingers. Even hearing Simeon's name gives me an instant headache, and I have no doubts that she would, in fact, tie me to a chair if I don't solve this issue soon.

Simeon has been asking for the first ten chapters of my next release, which wouldn't be a problem if I *had them*. I don't exactly know how to explain that the novel I've been working on for six months consists of a total of 93 words. I've tried to tell myself that it's not a lost cause, but lately, I can't think of anything I want less than to write this damn book.

"Oh, yeah." Janelle brushes her hair over one shoulder, waving her index finger in the air. "He wanted me to let you know to *stop avoiding him.*"

I groan, tossing my head backward and staring briefly at the lobby ceiling. It's painted with fish, and seashells, and anyone else from the city would call it tacky, but to me, it's the perfect, whimsical welcome.

"I can't do this right now," I mutter, shaking my head as if that will make all my problems disappear, like a mental Etch-A-Sketch.

"You good, Marc?" Janelle places a comforting hand on my shoulder, and I let out a sigh that's louder than I intended. She starts patting me, like she's consoling an eight-year-old who just lost the spelling bee. "You'll get those pages done, I'm sure of it. I can help you if—"

"It's not that," I cut in quickly. "Well, it *is*, but also..." An even louder exhale escapes my lips, and I look down at the floor, completely and utterly defeated.

"Damn. What the *hell* happened at that bookstore?"

A sad laugh slips from my lips. "You don't want to know."

We stand there in silence for a minute, taking up space in the hotel lobby like we're the only ones in the world to exist. Then, after a lingering moment, the familiar tingling sensation of acrylic nails scrapes against the top of my shoulder.

"You know what you need?" Janelle asks peppily. I look up at her, ready to mindlessly follow whatever her suggestion may be. I would really love the opportunity to remove my brain from my body right now. To not have to think about deadlines, and book tours, and ex-lovers. "You need a gin and tonic."

Janelle and I don't go to our rooms to freshen up. Instead, she marches me straight to the hotel bar, and sits me down on a worn wooden stool.

"A gin and tonic for him, and a margarita for me. On the rocks, extra salt please." Her gaze falls onto mine as she pulls out her card to pay. "It's on me," she smiles. I look down at the rectangular piece of plastic gripped between her fingers, and furrow my brows.

"That's your business card," I say flatly, though I can feel the corners of my lips defying gravity. Janelle sucks her lips into her mouth, then pops them loudly.

"Right. So its on me, *on you*." She smiles sheepishly, and I roll my eyes.

"You're lucky you're a good assistant so I let you get away with this shit."

Her arm shoves playfully into mine.

"*You're* lucky I'm a good assistant so I *don't* let you get away with shit."

I nod silently in agreement, and milliseconds after the bartender sets my drink in front of me, I begin to suck it down. Janelle, on the other hand, carefully slides the stem of her glass between her fingers and twirls it slowly. When I reach the bottom of the cup, and the obnoxious sound of straw-sucking-ice greets us, she sets her heavy glass back onto the bar.

"Excuse me," a familiar voice behind me utters. "Mr. Lovett?"

For a moment, my stomach turns into a solid mass, gravity pulling it straight to the floor. I've always tried to keep at least a small sense of anonymity, so I'm not accustomed to being recognized in public. Sure, I get occasionally identified by those who have met me at signings, but I don't think I've done an event within a 500-mile radius of this place. Janelle is on edge too, her gaze shooting to the person behind me and her body stiffening. I turn around quickly, before she goes all "body guard", and a wave of relief washes over my body when my eyes land on him.

"Hey! Umh..." I pause, trying to remember the Uber driver's name. He smiles.

"EJ," he answers, then places his palm on the back of the stool next to me.

Please don't sit down.

With a concerned look still planted on her face, Janelle shoots me a wide-eyed glance. I nod inconspicuously to ease her anxieties that we've been stalked by some murderous super-fan. Though, I'm confident her ill-considered fears are due to a massive miscommunication.

It seems, sometimes, that Janelle believes my desire to fly under the radar is because I'm scared of being stalked, or in the public eye. And while I enjoy my privacy, that couldn't be further from the truth. However, since I'm not one to divulge personal information, Janelle stands by her original assessment.

"It's like Selena or something, y'know?" she said once. "You never know who could be putting a target on your head."

"Didn't her employee kill her?" I asked, not looking up from my computer. Janelle pondered it for a second, before turning back to her manuscript.

"Oh. Yeah."

"Do you mind if I sit here?" EJ asks, his thin fingers dancing over the top of the stool. I turn to look at him, and offer him a smile that I pray looks real.

"Sure."

EJ seats himself beside me, waving the bartender down. "Whiskey, neat," he says deeply. Then his thumb points to me. "And whatever he's having."

My face flushes, and I wait for the burning sensation in my cheeks to subside before turning back to EJ.

"Oh, you don't have to do tha—"

"I looked you up," he cuts in. "Right after you hopped out of my car."

I swallow, a dry lump forming in the base of my throat. I have no idea why I feel nervous.

"Y-You did?"

He nods. "And I started reading one of your books."

I glance over at Nellie, who wriggles her eyebrows at me.

"Which one?" I ask, my voice cracking uncomfortably. EJ's hand creeps over to my stool's backrest, the heat from his arm burning into my spine.

I wasn't sure at first, but that definitely confirmed it. This man is hitting on me.

"The Jones Diary," he answers lowly.

Fuck me. Out of all the books he could have chosen, of course it happens to be the most raunchy, and poorly-written one of them all. The deadline for that was *six months*, and if I remember correctly, I was coping with a *lot* of sexual frustration at the time. Now, it's my turn to shoot Nellie an anxious glance.

"I have to admit," he continues, leaning closer to me so that his arm grazes against my back. "I was surprised to see how quickly you got down to it. I mean really, the first page? But it's good stuff, Carsen. *Really good.*"

Normally, I'd be flattered. A little put off, sure, but flattered. EJ is an attractive guy, and I'm not above turning down casual sex, even with a fan. But somehow, for what seems to be the first time ever, I am simply uninterested. Annoyed, even, though I'd never show it. I look over at Nellie, who seems to be completely sucked into her phone.

Great.

"It was really great seeing you again, EJ," I say, forcing an uncomfortable smile. "But I actually need to have a conversation with my assistant here." At her mention, Nellie's head shoots up, and she quickly tucks her phone into her lap. EJ nods, his thick dark brows weaving together in a disappointed fashion. "But I'll see you tomorrow at the signing, yeah?"

EJ smiles, then pats my back roughly as he slides his stool backwards.

"Of course," he says, reaching for his drink. He tips it in my direction, then winks. "Sorry for interrupting."

His eyes don't stop staring at me as he walks around to the other end of the bar, finding a seat amongst a group of people I can only assume he knows well. When his gaze finally breaks from mine, I look over at Janelle, overwhelmingly unamused. Her dark brown eyes bore into mine as she takes a long, uninterrupted swig of her drink.

"Are you going to tell me what's going on, or do I need to play twenty questions?" she asks with a sigh. My brows furrow, and I scoot the drink EJ purchased for me to the side.

"To what are you referring?" I ask, feigning ignorance. Nellie rolls her eyes so intensely, I'm scared for a moment, that they're going to get stuck.

"Don't pull that shit with me, Marcus. You just turned down a man— *no*— very *hot* man, who was *clearly* hitting on you." She grabs my sleeve, and her brow cocks, completely skeptical. "You have never turned down sex with a hot man. Hell, you *rarely* turn down sex with ugly ones."

"Janelle!" I exclaim embarrassedly through clenched teeth. "Could you *not?*"

Janelle waves a dismissive hand in the air.

"Oh please. You write smut for a living. It's *fine,* Marcus. It's research. Nobody cares."

I drag EJ's rejected drink in front of me, the glass emitting a smooth sound against the sleek bar-top. Janelle, again, starts pushing.

"Is it Simeon?" she asks. "Because if it's about Simeon, I can—"

"It's not Simeon."

"Okay..." She drags the word out, until it falls away. We sit in silence, the background noise of the bar filling in the space around us, until

Janelle clears her throat, and the tiny thread holding my jaw shut snaps.

"There was this guy," I blurt out quickly, before even realizing the words are mine. Nellie's body language finally loosens, a silent gesture to show she's listening. I shake my head, but continue anyway. "Not *a* guy." I correct. "*Kane.* His name was Kane." I stare into my glass, watching the miniscule bubbles float to the top.

"Okay," she says comfortingly. "Tell me about Kane."

I laugh, running a hand through my hair. I don't even know who Kane *is.* Truly, he's a stranger to me. Just some man I knew, for one summer, twenty years ago. A man I fell in love with, sure. But he's not the same person now, and neither am I. Everyone changes as time goes on. I know nothing about the Kane alive today, so I have nothing to say. But memories from that summer flood my mind, filling my senses. I can almost smell the coconut cologne he wore, and hear the deep tones of his somber voice trickling over me. It's like I'm breathing in the taste of his lips, sea salt and pineapple tingling my tastebuds.

But if there's one thing I remember the most, it's that Kane is one giant contradiction. He's like dancing in a thunderstorm. Like tea gone cold, but so sweet you add ice instead of tossing it. He's the last day of summer, when it's too cold to swim, but you lay on the beach anyway to soak in the last rays of the sun.

"Do you remember when you asked if I ever actually *date*?" I ask, fidgeting with the thin black straw in my fizzy drink. Janelle nods.

"Yeah. You said you only ever dated—" She gasps. "Oh my god! He's the one! Is he the one?"

I suck my lips into my mouth, biting down on them as I nod.

"Yeah."

After I hired Janelle, it didn't take long for us to begin confiding in one another. Or, rather, her prying my own private information out of me, then dumping her own on top for added pleasure. Her pleasure, of course. A few months into having her by my side, she picked up on my hookup routine, and tried to set me up on a real date. She refused to cancel it unless I explained why I don't "do relationships", so reluctantly, I did.

I went into every detail. I told her about Chance, dragging me into Well Written Books after a summer swim, bumping me right into Kane like a scene from a romance novel. I told her about how irritated he was that a wet dog was in the store, and how he became much *more* irritated when I asked if they were hiring. I told her about our first kiss, and the night we made love in the lighthouse. And of course, then, I told her, about how I fucked it all up. How when people found out about us, no matter how hard I tried to hide it, word got back to my parents. And worst of all, how I up and moved across the country, without ever seeing Kane again.

I don't date, because I had love, and I ran from it. And while I may be unmemorable, what we had, that feeling we shared? It could never truly be forgotten.

"Here." Nellie shoves the untouched gin and tonic across the bar. "You need something stronger than that." Her gaze flicks up to the bartender, and she slaps her palms together. "Four shots of tequila, please!"

a bottle of gin
is nauseatingly sweet
compared to every moment
that i am not with you
-MF

Chapter Five

KANE

"God dammit!" I lunge for the fancy water dispenser, but it topples to the ground just as the tips of my fingers graze it. The plastic stays unscathed, but the lid pops off, flying halfway across the store and flooding the entire area within a three foot radius. Instead of doing the adult thing and grabbing towels, I stay sat on the floor, burying my face in my hands.

Clara rushes from the storage room, her arms piled high with a stack of Lovett's— or should I say *Marcus'*— newest release.

"Shit, Kane! Are you okay?" she asks worriedly, setting the books aside and rushing up to me. I huff.

"I give up," I say flatly, which is a phrase that often leaves my mouth when anything goes even slightly awry. I don't need to look at Clara to know she is frowning. I know from experience.

"You're not ending it over spilt water, Kane."

I huff loudly again, but grab her hand and allow her to help me up. Unbeknownst to Clara, the water is simply the tipping point today, not the main aggressor. If she knew the real reason behind my absurdly high stress levels, she'd probably shit her pants.

Still, I need to tell her.

Clara was there, for all of it. Okay, not *all of it*. But she was there for the important parts. The day I met Marcus, she came over after work, and I ranted to her about the hot dude dragging seawater through the store. I crashed on her couch the night Marcus first kissed me, then practically lived on it after he left. When Clara finds out Marcus is Carsen V. Lovett, she might just strangle him with her bare hands.

"Go sit behind the desk and do inventory for the party. I'll clean this up," she instructs. I open my mouth to protest, but she doesn't give me the opportunity. "Just do it, Kane."

I sigh, dragging my feet on the way to the giant stack of books written by the World's Biggest Dick. Clara disappears into the stock room, then quickly returns with a stack of towels.

"Are you getting cold feet?" she asks as she drapes them over the puddle. "It's completely normal to be nervous."

I chew on the inside of my cheek, and continue staring at the glossy, hardcovers towering over me. It feels like they're planning an ambush.

"I'm not getting cold feet."

The squishing sound of wet towels beneath her shoes causes both of our faces to wrinkle, and Clara crosses her arms assertively.

"Okay. Are you just... having a day then? It's okay if you're having a day. I didn't expect you to be *magically cured* just because you're meeting your Book Daddy."

"Oh my *god. N*ever, *ever* say that again," I groan, but Clara giggles. "I'm serious, Claire. That's— just *no*."

"Alright, alright." She surrenders. "Can I do anything to help?"

I shake my head. "I have to tell you something," I confess. One of the things I love about Clara, is how much she loves others. But because of that, I have a sneaking suspicion that she might take the news even harder than I did. I was shocked. Propelled out of reality for a good couple minutes. But Clara? Oh Clara is going to be *pissed.* We'll be lucky if we make it through the launch party without her threats of dismantling his success or ripping his dick off.

"And what is that, Sugar Kane?"

"I—" I stop, gathering up the courage, and vocabulary, to explain the absolute shit show that is going to be this launch party. But just as the words start to piece together in my mind, the worst sound known to any dog owner makes every other thought in my head disappear.

Gagging. *Retching.* This strange, bubbling sound coming from the inside of Dickie's abdomen. Clara's eyes lock on mine, she too recognizing the foul song of Dickie's breakfast, traveling up his esophagus. We work together like trained agents, me racing to Dickie, and her following quickly behind with a sopping-wet towel, a tiny trail of water marking the path behind us.

Dickie vomits just as I reach him, and both Clara and I recoil at the rancid odor. The chime of a bell pierces the sour air, and the front door to Well Written Book swings open, casting a ray of sunlight directly onto Clara, Dickie, me, and the fresh pile of vomit between us.

"Happy launch day!" Marcus announces proudly. But the beaming smile on his face drops almost instantly, as either the sight, or scent, fills his senses. Instinctively, I look at Clara. Clara looks at Marc, and Marc looks at me, then Clara, like a comedic, cinematic move from the universe.

Oh fuck.

Marcus narrows his gaze at Clara, but not before she fixates her own gaze onto *him*. I jump up quickly, unsure of what exactly to do in this situation. Explain to Clara? Apologize to Marcus for the vomit? Rub his smug little face in it?

"What the fuck?!" Clara jolts up, a stack of creases forming on her brow as she narrows her eyes accusingly onto Marcus. "Is that—" She turns to me, but doesn't give me the opportunity to respond before she continues speaking. "No it can't— are you? You're?" She waves her hands in circles at Marcus, and it looks as though she may pass out. I wrap my arm around her waist to steady her.

"Okay." I guide her to the chair behind the desk as she continues to bitterly mutter incoherent sentences. "*You* sit *here*, and I'm going to clean that up. *You*—" I point at Marcus, who looks like a schoolboy caught drawing penises on the desks. He throws his hands up in defense, his grey brows shooting to his hairline. "Sit—" I glance around the room. "Sit over there. And do *not* speak to her."

Marcus does as he's told, and I quickly clean up Dickie's spent breakfast, spraying the area with a generous amount of air freshener afterward. I look over at Clara, who appears to be attempting to burn holes through Marcus' skull with her eyes. Marcus looks terrified, staring at the ceiling to avoid eye contact.

"I like the chandeliers," he says nonchalantly. I follow his gaze to a vintage, candelabra-style chandelier swaying gently between bookshelves. Clara picked that one out at the Coral Beach flea market. Later that day, she called me crying in a Target bathroom, begging me to pick her up because she just found out she was pregnant.

Clara *loves* that chandelier.

"You have some fucking nerve—" She stands up from her seat, her face growing a shade of red so dark I'm sure I should be worried.

"Clara!" I snap. Her gaze flicks over to me, and I shake my head. "Please, can we *please* just be adults about this? It was twenty years ago."

"Time doesn't make you less of a dickwad," she spits at Marcus, who still sits there awkwardly with his hands in his lap like a gentleman.

To be fair, she's right. Time doesn't make you less of a dickwad, only change does. And I have no knowledge, nor desire for knowledge, that Marcus Fraund is a changed man. Regardless, we have a business to run. And there is no way in hell I am refunding seventy tickets to this stupid fucking launch party.

I don't know whether or not he deserves it, but I still offer Marcus a genuinely apologetic look. It's not like he knew this entire mess would happen. When his eyes catch mine from across the room, my breath hitches. I look back to Clara.

"I was trying to tell you," I explain.

"Tell me what? That this *asshole* is back in town?"

"That I'm Carsen V. Lovett," Marcus announces, standing up. How he manages to look so regal in such a disastrous situation is beyond me, but I try not to pay too much attention to it. I expect Clara to yell, or maybe let out The Scoff Heard Around the World. Instead, cackling, maniacal laughter seeps from her open mouth and rumbles throughout the building. Her palm slaps against the desk so hard, it had to have hurt. But Clara doesn't even flinch. She just keeps laughing.

"He's joking, right?" she manages to squeak, tears pricking her eyes as she doubles over. Marcus shoots me a concerned glance, and I chew on my lower lip, embarrassment creeping over me. I don't know why I'm embarrassed. Clara's cackling like Ursula the Sea Witch, Marcus showed up expecting a simple, nostalgic book launch, and Dickie's the one who threw up. Still, heat begins to flood my cheeks, and I drag a hand over my mouth, shaking my head.

"You know, we used to be friends, Clara," Marcus says. Then, if its humanly possible, Clara laughs louder. Marcus points to her with a concerned expression. "Is she..."

I nod sheepishly. "Yeah, no, she's fine. It's just— she might kill you, is all."

Marcus nods acceptingly. "Fair." He waves. "Nice to see you again, Claire."

Abruptly, Clara stands up, and walks silently, and straight-faced, back to the storage room, Dickie trailing behind her.

"She didn't get a warning," I explain awkwardly. Marcus approaches me, my heart thrumming harder against the inside of my ribcage with each step closer.

"Neither did you," he says, his voice deep and buttery. I swallow, an ache forming in the base of my throat.

"Yeah, well..." I clear my throat. "Like I said, it was twenty years ago." That statement comes off really mature for someone who was just picturing rubbing his ex's face in dog vomit. "We should get ready. We open soon."

Marcus nods, rubbing his palms together. "You got it. What can I help with?"

I shake my head.

"You're the guest," I say through gritted teeth. Meeting Carsen V. Lovett has been at the top of my bucket list for over a decade. It's crazy how quickly things can change.

Lovett could've been anyone. Seven billion people on this stupid fucking planet, and it just *had* to be him. And this launch party, this sweet, wholesome gesture from my favorite person, has become my literal hell.

Marcus glances around the room curiously, his eyes landing on the mess by the concessions table. Wet towels piled up next to the plastic water dispenser. He strolls over, gathering the towels into his arms.

"Where do I put them?"

"I'll take them," I say, offering my arms out. But Marcus doesn't budge. "Marcus, these need to go into the back room. If I send you in there with Clara still seething, you might never make it out."

The stupidly charming smile that Marcus has plastered on his face falters, and he reluctantly hands the sopping pile over. I carry them to the storage room, knowing full and well, that I am going to look like an absolute soaking mess when I set them down.

"How the hell are you so calm?" Clara practically lunges at me the second I walk through the door. I toss the towels into a plastic tote bag, making a mental note to bring them home tonight and wash them. I shrug.

"I just do not have the energy to care," I respond truthfully. Well, *mostly* truthfully. I don't have the energy to care, but that doesn't stop me from feeling it. It doesn't prevent that aching, stinging sensation from consuming my body when I'm transported back to that summer.

Like I told Marcus, it was twenty years ago. So why the hell does it still have such a strong fucking grip on me?

"Did you know?" Clara asks accusingly, her eyes squinting in my direction. I shake my head.

"Just found out yesterday," I answer.

"Do you want me to make him leave?" She brushes a strand of hair out of my face, then cups my cheek gently. "I'll kick that asshole out of here, and make him pay for everything plus emotional damages."

A soft chuckle escapes my mouth, and I lean into her touch. "Claire, you're my best friend. And if that's what I wanted, you know you'd be the first person I'd ask." She nods in approval, her soft fingertips rubbing against my cheek. "But the easiest way for me to deal with this is to just get through it, with as little bumps possible."

Clara offers me an angelic smile.

"Okay," she agrees, pulling away. "I'll be civil."

"Thank you." I turn toward the door, pulling it open.

"Kane?" she asks. I look over my shoulder at her.

"Yes?"

"I'm sorry your Book Daddy ended up being your shitty ex." Clara bites her bottom lip to hold in a laugh, and an aching smile betrays me.

"Thanks, Clara."

Seventy people doesn't sound like a lot, until they're all crammed into a tiny seaside bookstore. I was ecstatic when Clara told me the numbers, but now that everyone is actually here, I just feel overwhelmed.

And hot. *Very* hot.

I guess I should be grateful that Marcus' work is so renowned, because the sea of people dividing us is so vast that if I weren't already aware, I'd have no idea we were in the same room. Loud chatter fills every crevice of the store, until it feels as if there's no space left for me.

It's a feeling I'm accustomed to, even when living in pure silence. I'm not sure there's ever been a time where I felt like I belonged. As a kid, I'd stand awkwardly to the side at the park, watching as all the other children talked and played and argued. During my teenage years, I didn't even attempt to attend any dances, because I knew I'd converse with nobody but my English teacher, and wind up leaving thirty minutes in. Even in my relationship with Clara, it felt like there was no space for me. Not because of anything she did, or said, but because I'm positive that my profound misery poisons all the air in the room. That Clara had to hold her breath for seventeen years, and one day, she'd suffocate.

This was supposed to be it.

This was supposed to be the one day, the few hours of my life where I felt like, for once, I understood the people around me, and they understood me. Now, I feel more lost than ever.

It doesn't make sense, Marcus being Lovett. Lovett crafting the most intense and passionate queer stories, and those stories resembling something we lived together long ago. It doesn't make sense, and yet, it's the most sensible thing in the world.

All the coincidences, the tiny easter eggs. I thought—

Well, I guess I don't know what I thought. That every sad, gay person goes through the same, unbearable breakups? That they all love people who hate themselves?

It should have clicked. I loved reading the stray notes Marcus left scattered about the store. He'd tuck them into the cracks of the shelves, and between pages of my favorite books. It was like a treasure hunt, gems of his thoughts and feelings, tied together with a literary string. I used to collect them, and keep them in a blue book-shaped box. Sometimes when he spoke, it sounded like he was born two-hundred years late. Nothing so beautiful could be so modern, and yet, there he was.

It feels so twisted for Marcus to be gifted at the thing I love most. He was born to write, and I was made to read every single word.

"Okay!" Clara's voice travels through the buzzing crowd, but it appears, likely due to recognition, that I am the only one who heard it. "Alright!" she says again, but still, it remains futile.

A sharp, thunderous clap shoots through the air, followed by an amplified, domineering voice.

"Listen up!" the woman snaps, but the smile on her face makes the irritated tone appear feigned. She points a pink acrylic nail at Clara, who offers her a sincere, satisfied gleam.

"Thank you," Clara blushes, then clears her throat loudly. "Mar—*Sorry*. Mr. *Lovett* will now be reading a highly-anticipated excerpt from *The Thread Untied*. If you will all please find your seats." She gestures to various areas in the store, with additional, provisional seating. "There's more spots over *there,* and... over *here,* thank you. I will now turn you over to Mr. Lovett."

I have to hand it to her. Despite her burning hatred toward Marcus, she's been handling this event extremely well. Even if she does spit out his name like its bitter on her tastebuds. I, on the other hand, am channeling all of my anxious energy into Dickie's midday back scratches. He's rather pleased, I'm sure, by the way his legs stretch out in front of him, his little toes separating into tiny pink jellybeans.

All the noise in the room begins to die down, but I don't realize just how quiet it is until something else takes its place. It's difficult to fathom how one voice can feel larger than seventy. How one person can feel infinitely more intimidating. I don't want to be here. And even more, I do not want to hear a single word to come from Marcus' stupid mouth. So why do I inch closer, holding my breath so the sound of air doesn't fill my ears?

"Firstly, I just want to thank all of you for being here. I know you have so many choices to make, when spending your time and hard-earned money, and I am so grateful that you decided to be here with me today." His eyes scan the room, and a gentle smile tugs at his lips. "I guess I should get to it, then."

I shouldn't want to look at Marcus. Every second of his presence is just a painful reminder of how lonely life was after he left. Him being Lovett was a cue to solidify my belief that nobody else really understood me, it was him all along. But it's so hard not to notice all of the miniscule differences to the way I once remembered him. So my eyes stay glued, and I continue scooting closer to get a better look.

Gentle creases line the skin above his high cheekbones, making the amount of time we've been apart much more uncomfortably real. All the years together we surrendered. I wonder what jokes formed the rays next to his eyes, and what worries triggered the shallow valleys around his lips. I wonder if someone else's fingers get to stroke his greying hair each night as his mind wanders aimlessly, pulling words from the abyss to form stories I've been secretly desperate for.

"Walter's lips graze the delicate shell of my ear, each hair on my body standing as if they're reaching out for him to touch," Marcus reads. Just as my gaze shifts from his hair to his eyes, Marcus' deep blue eyes lock onto mine. It's like the planet Neptune itself, silently dissecting every bit of me from across the room. "'I want you,' he whispers."

you are the ink
that seeps into the pages
of every world i create
and in those stories
the universes themselves
we are not a sin
but a miracle of divinity

-MF

Chapter Six

MARCUS

My gaze is glued to the soft, cream pages of *The Thread Untied*. Partially because that's how reading works, but largely due to the fact that every time they look away, they seem to find Kane sitting at the back of the crowd. Why the hell did I choose to read an excerpt so *graphic*?

"'I groan at the sensation of his skin grazing mine. The soft tickle of the hair below his navel drags down my stomach as his head lowers to my— to my...'"

I clear my throat, blood rushing to the tops of my cheeks. My face burns as my eyes scan the word over and over again. Something flashes in my mind. A distant memory, of trailing fingertips and soft gasps. Kane's breathy whispers, begging me for more. God, I hate myself.

"My cock."

I break my stare at the word to glance at Janelle. Her brows furrow in concern, and she quickly replaces the book in my hand with a cup of water. I gulp it down, then exhale slowly through my nose.

"Sorry," I chuckle nervously. "I seem to be getting a bit overheated."

"Because it's steamy in here!" someone calls out suggestively from the crowd. My gaze flashes over to the familiar stranger, EJ wearing a proudly indicative smirk. He shoots me a wink, and the warmth in my cheeks intensifies.

I always read smut at my launch parties. It's what I'm known for, mostly. I like to think there are some who see my work deeper than that, but I don't mind that it's the average person's focus. Sex sells, and for good reason. It can mean so many things beyond animalistic instincts and divine pleasure. But it also doesn't have to. I've never had a problem reading it aloud, because it's such a natural thing. But today, I find myself struggling with the words in front of me, and I'm going to pretend that I have no idea why.

"And that's it!" Nellie announces, slamming the book shut. "If you want to know what happens next, grab a signed copy before you leave! And don't forget to thank Clara and Kane for welcoming us into their beautiful store."

Indiscernible mumbles come from the crowd in front of me, which gradually transforms into a confused round of applause. My eyes shift to my fans, and I stand up, forcing a thankful grin.

"Thank you, everyone. Really, thank you so much." I place my hand on my chest, the heavy thrum of my heart vibrating to my fingertips. My eyes filter through the crowd until they find what they're so desperately searching for. Kane stares at me, his lips slightly parted, and his cheeks flushed.

At least I am not the only victim of my poor excerpt decision, though I think it might be better if I were. The second he realizes I'm looking at him, his jaw snaps shut. I gesture a hand toward him, then one at Clara, who I swear is plotting some sort of assassination.

"And again, the most sincere gratitude for our hosts today. Feel free to stick around and browse their collections. I wouldn't be here without them."

Kane's warm, chestnut eyes grow round as my words travel to him. His head begins to tilt, but as I stand, ready to approach him, I'm flooded with hounding questions, reaching hands, and a sea of bodies.

"Step back please!" Janelle commands, inserting herself between me and the crowd. "You will all have a chance to speak with Carsen at the signing table. And no physical contact, or Derrick here will toss you out!" Clara's husband beams proudly next to her, and though he's undeniably large enough to play bodyguard, something about the softness of his grin makes me feel like I'd be better off with Clara herself.

"Now, line up!"

After what feels like years, the crowd begins to dwindle, and my wrist starts cramping from the repeated dance of my signature. I don't mind it, really. It's worth it to know that so many people, in the very town I was condemned, celebrate the kind of love I write about. Coral Beach was never inherently homophobic, but it wasn't necessarily supportive either. Growing up, there was always a sharp line dividing the city.

Those who embraced it, and those who didn't.

For the longest time, I was the latter, for no other reason than the simple fact that my parents were the same. And even if he hates me, I'll always love Kane. Because if I hadn't met him, I think hatred would have consumed me. Externally. Internally.

"Are your erotic scenes inspired by real life?"

I take moment to control my facial muscles, before looking up at the person who just spoke. EJ grins eagerly, sliding his copy of my novel across the table for me to sign. I force an uncomfortable smile, but a telling sigh slips out of me.

"Nope."

I scribble my signature extra messily on the title page, then push the book back toward him. His shoulders sink down, and he almost rolls his eyes as he leaves the line. *Jesus.* Has the guy ever heard of *manners?*

"Next!" Nellie yells, right next to my ear. The aggressive sound of gum smacking quickly follows, and I almost shoot her a dirty look, but it stops abruptly when the next person in line steps forward. I choke, on air or spit or regret, and Nellie slides another cup of water toward me.

"Are you okay?" Kane asks, but his brow is cocked in a way that tells me he isn't *too* concerned. Like maybe, if I wasn't okay, he would be perfectly content. My head bounces as I nod violently, until I feel the point of an elbow jab into my ribcage. My gaze shifts to Janelle, and I shoot her an irritated glance until I realize that she's trying to *help me.* Her head shakes inconspicuously, her dark brown eyes wide and round with embarrassment. The second-hand kind. My cheeks puff as I blow out a steady stream of air, before turning back to Kane.

"Oh." I wave my hands around dismissively. "Yeah. I'm good. All good. You?"

With his eyebrow still judging me, Kane slides a pristine, hardcover copy of *The Thread Untied* across the table. My pulse quickens, and I stare at it curiously for a moment, before looking back up at him.

"You... want a signed copy?" A nervous laugh bubbles out of me, but Kane's expression doesn't shift. His hands, however, jam into his pockets so far down that the waistline of his pants rolls slightly. Barely, but just enough that a tiny strip of skin below his stomach exposes itself, and the thick, dark hairs growing from it, creep out as well. I suck in a quick breath, forcing my gaze to move anywhere but down.

"They're worth more signed, so—" Kane shrugs, then shakes his head softly so that his messy brown waves move out of his eyes. "If you don't mind."

"I don't."

I smile, and I'm surprised when I see that Kane smiles back. He doesn't smile by habit. Or at least, he didn't back then. It was a rare occurrence, but a magnificent one, because when it happened, you knew it was real. A pure and honest display of his fleeting emotion, something to be cherished. I wonder if it's the same now. I'm sure, as he's aged, he's fallen into the same politeness as the rest of us. To put on the mask that everything is swell. But despite the lines surrounding the smile, it looks just as it did twenty years ago, so I cherish it anyway.

"Do you just want me to sign it, or..." I trail off, and in my brain, I'm bashing my forehead into the table. Kane chews on his lower lip, his gaze moving around me, but never looking at me directly.

"You could personalize it," he says softly. "If you want. Anything is okay."

I nod, this time ensuring I'm aware of both the duration and velocity. My fingers find the divot between the cover and the pages, and I flip the book open, smoothing my palm over the title page to flatten it. I want this to be perfect.

Yet I have no idea what to say.

The page stares back, the title inked across it taunting me. *The Thread Untied*. And suddenly, I get an idea.

I'm going to regret this.

Really, it's a terrible idea. But this can't be the last time I see Kane. I have to talk to him. I need to apologize. My fingers pick up the marker beside me, and I begin to scribble words carefully across the page.

The shutters are white. They were brown before, which I always thought was ugly, but they're white now, and for some reason, I don't really like that either. It doesn't even look like my childhood home anymore. Not just because of the colors, but the add-on, and the balcony, and the aura.

I'm glad it bears little resemblance, actually, because if it looked the same, I'd believe my parents still lived there. They were never big on accepting change. Still, I never allowed myself to wonder where they may have gone. Are they alive, even? Most likely. But I know the best course of action is to keep pretending they aren't. Twenty years ago, I died. To them at least, and they to me. It's funny how many conditions come with unconditional love.

Religion. Career. Sexuality.

And I am nothing if not an overachiever, so of course, I went three-for-three.

A vibrating sensation rumbles in my pocket, and I pull out my phone, reading the name dancing across the screen.

Oh fuck.

I thought Janelle's description of my supposed illness would at least keep Simeon away for a couple more days. But I think he's running out of patience, and I'm undoubtedly running out of excuses. I take a steadying breath, roll my shoulders back, and press the phone to my ear.

"Marc," I announce. I can hear some scrambling through the receiver, like Simeon wasn't prepared for me to actually answer.

"Marcus?"

"I'm here, Simeon," I reply. My ear is filled with more indiscernible sounds, before finally becoming clear again.

"Hi Marcus." Simeon clears his throat. "Can you talk? Please?"

I stare at the nearly unrecognizable house across the street, lingering for a moment. I don't know why I'm drawn toward it rather than away. Still, I spin on my heel, and begin my walk back to the inn.

"Yeah," I say. "I can talk."

"Great!" A pause of silence follows the word, and I prepare myself for the professional and passive wrath of Simeon Goldberg. He lets out a long sigh. "Look, Marc. I have to be honest with you. I'm not the big boss, here. I'm just the little guy. And my job, as the *little guy*, is to deliver a completed manuscript to the publishers, by the *due date*."

I pinch the inner corners of my eyes between my thumb and index finger, breathing out slowly.

"Yeah, I know Simeon." I try not to let my distaste for the guilt-approach present itself in my tone. "I'm sorry it's taking so long, it's just- it's not working for me. I'm not connecting with the characters like I thought I was going to, and I just— I think I need to scrap it. Start a new one, maybe."

Simeon clears his throat on the other end of the phone, and I pull it away from my ear so I can sigh as loudly as I want without moral repercussions.

"There is no 'scrapping it', Marcus. This is the book the you signed the deal for. This is the book we have to deliver. *In three months.* You *had* six. Frankly, Marc, my highschooler could finish a book in that time frame."

"I'll get the pages to you, Simeon," I say flatly, and I pat myself on the back for simply clicking the red button to end the call, rather than chucking my phone onto the concrete slabs in front of me.

"How was your walk?" Nellie greets me at the door of the hotel, like she somehow knew when exactly I'd arrive. I nod at her in appreciation as I step inside, but forget to fight the exasperated sigh that flattens my lungs.

"Simeon called," I explain. She nods, because that, of course, is explanation enough. Then, a beaming smile conquers her face.

"You—" She grabs my bicep, and begins dragging me toward the stairs. "—have other things to focus on right now."

I pause on the steps, feeling her grip tighten around my arm. "Like what?"

Nellie rolls her eyes. "Uh, like your date? You know, the invite you scribbled into Kane's book? At seven?"

I step back, the metal railing of the staircase catching my fall.

"It's not a date," I say firmly. Again, she rolls her eyes. "And besides, it's not like he's going to show."

She huffs, grabbing my arm again and pulling me up the rest of the way, until we reach the door to my hotel room.

"You're being very..." Her hands wave around like she's casting a spell on me. "I don't know, annoying? *Pouty*. You're being very pouty. Open the door."

I don't know why I listen to Janelle. Maybe because every time I feel like my career is falling apart, she swoops in to fix it. Or maybe, it's just nice sometimes to be told what to do. In any event, the door swings open, and she wastes no time finding my suitcase and digging through it. I stand behind her, watching as all of my carefully folded clothes become wadded balls of wrinkled linen. Finally, she turns to me, her cheeks glowing with a radiant smile.

"Put this on," she commands. Reluctantly, I take the outfit into the bathroom, and begin to change.

The pants she chose are new. *New*, new. Like, I haven't even tried them on, new. They look kind of small, and I'm nervous, because if they don't fit, I'll just take it as a sign that this was, in fact, a terrible idea. My eyes close as I slide on the pants, the textured feel of linen dragging against my bare legs causes goosebumps to wash over them. When I blindly find the inner metal clasp, and lock the pieces together, I suck in a shaky breath.

They fit.

I open my eyes and grab the shirt of Janelle's choice; a worn blue button up. It's old, *years* old, and honestly, I'm not even sure why I still own it, much less why I brought it all the way here. Anxiously, I pull my arms through the sleeves, and begin to button it.

This was a really, really bad idea. Why did I do this? Why did I even come to Coral Springs in the first place?

I stare into the mirror as my thoughts spiral. It actually is a pretty good outfit. The colors are soft and beachy, the textures loose and flattering. I run a comb through my hair one, two, three too many times, then follow it with my fingers, the grey hairs moving to create a path of their own direction.

"Hurry up, I want to see!" Nellie calls out through the closed door. If I don't come out now, I'll probably stay in this bathroom until I die. So I take a breath, shake my hair around one last time, then open the bathroom door, and step out.

Nellie's face lights up, and I swear to god there's a twinkle in her eye. She gasps.

"*Oh.*" Her head nods aggressively, and her cheeks flush with a dark red hue. "He's gonna show up."

i never wore the color red
i thought it didn't flatter me
but when i found out
it's your favorite
i bought a scarlet polo
in hopes you'd look at me
                    -MF

Chapter Seven

KANE

I don't want babies. I don't want babies. I don't want babies.

Judah's ocean blue eyes bore into mine, and just as I mentally repeat the sentence for the fourth time, a toothless grin breaks across his face. It's so cute, I almost fucking *die*.

"Are you helping Uncle Kane?" Derrick signs from the kitchen. Judah doesn't take his eyes off me, not even for his father. Instead, a giggle that I can only compare to a kitten's hiccup slips from his chubby little mouth, and he grabs my nose aggressively.

"Ope—" Clara removes his hand from my face, then beckons Dickie onto her lap. "We're working on grabbing and hitting. Sorry."

I shrug, because who the hell could stay mad at something so squishy and innocent?

"So, let me get this straight," she continues, her tone filled with irritation. The speed in which she is petting Dickie quickens, though he doesn't seem to mind. "Marcus *ruined* your copy of his new book by scribbling some *stupid* invitation to meet him tonight in permanent marker?"

I keep staring at Judah to avoid eye contact with his mother.

"Yes."

"And you're *actually* considering going?"

I know Clara's pissed, so I suck my cheeks in and chew on the skin for a minute to create the illusion of hesitation.

"Yes," I answer finally.

She shakes her head, and seems like she's going to stay silent for a moment, but I know better than to think that's in her control. A quick, sharp breath zips through her clenched teeth, and I stay preoccupied with Judah as he grabs at my cheeks. He pulls the skin from one side to the other, contorting my face a million different ways to entertain himself.

"Are you hearing this Derrick?" she calls out

Derrick pokes his head up from behind the island, one hand on his hip and a spatula in the other.

"I'm still catching up." He waves the spatula around. "Why do we hate him, again?"

"Because he broke Kane's heart!" Clara exclaims, clapping her hands together. "Kane and Marcus dated in college."

"Right, I remember that part," Derrick says, turning back to the stove. He moves the spatula around in a circular motion, the scent of greasy ground beef and cumin wafting in the air around us. "But what did he... *do*?"

In my peripheral vision, I can see Clara glance at me, but I pretend I'm completely blind to it. This conversation might be about me, but I want no part in it. I don't care if Derrick knows the story, I just don't want to listen to it.

Why I'm even entertaining the idea of showing up is beyond me. I don't owe Marcus anything. Not a conversation, not a glance, not even the time of day. There is nothing I could gain from this meetup, except the one thing I've been craving.

A real, and genuine apology.

"Marcus' parents found out about them," Clara explains carefully. "Marc wasn't out, and his parents were... *yeah*. Anyway, the next day he was gone. No note, no call, nothing. His parents even showed up at the store, and accused Kane of—" She stops, like the words are caught in her throat. "They said he corrupted him. That Marcus *denied* the entire relationship, and claimed that Kane tried to push his 'lifestyle' on him. Fucking prick."

"Clara!" I shoot her wide-eyed glance, and cover Judah's ears. Her expression drops, looking at me condescendingly.

"He's deaf, Kane."

My cheeks flush embarrassedly, and I nod. "Right."

Derrick chuckles, steam flowing around his face as he stares sympathetically at me. This is the worst part. The pity.

I've been pitied my whole life. Everyone feels sorry for the kid who is diagnosed with clinical depression at age nine. The one who's put on antidepressants at ten, and hospitalized at twelve. I never knew how to explain to them that pitying me just made everything worse. I didn't want to be another thing in their life they had to feel sorry for. I just wanted to be normal.

I just wanted to be happy.

"It was twenty years ago," I remind him. Clara's gaze flashes to me, her brows weaved together with concern.

I know I've said it, but I love Clara. I really do. I just wish, sometimes, she would stop feeling sorry for me too, and let me exist in the reality I've been given. I've moved on, kind of. I've healed, mostly. I just want a goddamned apology.

"I think you should go," Derrick says casually, picking up the pan and placing it onto a potholder. Clara's head whips around, her face scrunched with surprised dissatisfaction.

"What?!"

He shrugs. "Yeah! I mean, *clearly* what happened would leave anyone with some damage. If Kane wants to go get an explanation, or an apology, or fuck, I don't know, *revenge*?" His eyes lock onto mine. "I'm with him."

Clara looks back and forth between Derrick and I, her eyes narrowing and her brows dropping lower.

"I knew I'd regret this *bond* you guys have," she mutters, but a slight smile tugs at the corners of her lips. Derrick approaches from the kitchen, wiping his palms down the front of his "kiss the cook" apron.

"Can I see it?" he asks. My brows furrow, and I look up at him, confused.

"See what?"

"The note!" He gestures his hands like his request was obvious. I hand Judah over to him, then grab my bag, pulling out the hardcover book.

It's gorgeous. Sleek, and glossy, a spool of golden, foil-plated thread illustrated on the front. The string dances across the cover, looping into different directions, but never forming a knot. I flip the front cover open, revealing the note Marcus left inside.

Kane

THE THREAD

Untied

What do you say we finally tie this thread? If you so desire, meet me at our spot at seven. Hope to see you there.

Carsen V. Lovett

I watch Derrick's eyes increasingly widen each time he re-reads it. I wonder if I had the same confused, and bewildered look on my face. Surely, mine was even worse.

"What do you think that means?" he asks, pointing to the note. "'Tie this thread'?"

I shrug, self-consciously pulling the book away from him.

"I think he's going to apologize," I answer. I try to fight it, but my gaze drifts to Clara, an unsurprisingly sour look settled onto her face.

"*Or,*" Derrick counters mischievously, wriggling his eyebrows. "He's trying to rekindle the flame."

Clara shoves him playfully, and heat rushes to the tops of my cheeks as I shake my head violently. There is nothing I want less than to entertain Marcus Fraund ever again. I hate him, truly. So it's strange that my stomach flutters as Derrick introduces the idea.

"That's not going to happen," I say pointedly, and Derrick shrugs.

"Probably not." He smiles. "But you'll die wondering if you don't go."

I swallow, my throat becoming dryer by the second as I think about it. As I ponder seeing Marcus' face again. As I watch his eyes move while he explains why he threw me under the bus, and disappeared without a single word. While he apologizes for hurting me, giving me the closure I've needed. My gut twists at the thought of finally having answers, and I think I might throw up. But Derrick is right.

If I don't go, I'll die wondering.

I hate that Marcus referred to Rita's as *"our place."* I mean, sure, it *was* our place. But first, it was *my* place. And after he left, I kept it as that.

To him, there's no difference. The beige netting hanging from the ceiling, buoys draped along the walls, the sounds of the ocean crashing through the open window along the back, they were all the same when it was ours. But I know the difference.

It's in the worn leather seats, and the sound of the atmosphere. In the scent of the grease, and the splintering grain in the tables. The dim lights hanging from the ceiling, and the taste of the food. Marcus' absence changed it all.

But there is one thing that has always remained.

My gaze draws to the booth in the back right corner of the restaurant. I've had hundreds of meals in that booth. Alone. With Clara. With Marcus. I've tried to sit elsewhere, trust me. But the dip in the cushion never felt right, and the bulb in the lamp above me shone right into my eye.

It's almost haunting, seeing Marcus sit there now, in the same seat across from mine. Memories begin to flood my mind, but I force them back. I didn't come here to reminisce.

I came here to heal.

"It had to be this booth?" I ask him as I approach the table. Marcus' focus abruptly shifts from his phone to me. He shoves the device quickly into his pocket, his pale cheeks flushing the color of a rose.

"I didn't think you were coming," he answers honestly, gesturing for me to take my seat. I slide into the bench across from him, wiping the palms of my hands against my pants.

"I don't know why I did." I pause, considering it. "Maybe I do."

Marcus' brows jump, and I wait for him to ask me the reason. Why, after everything, after all these years, did I decide to give him a single moment of my time. But he doesn't. Instead, he sticks his hand in the air, waving over the waitress, and plastering on a beaming grin.

"Are you ready to order?" the waitress asks. Marcus nods, sliding the laminated menu across the table toward me.

"I'll take a number two, no mayo. And, what's the largest size you offer for fries?"

The waitress glances at me, an uncomfortable expression sewn into the corners of her face.

"Umh...large?"

I look at Marcus, his eyes drifting to the ceiling as if he's deep in thought.

"Hm. Okay then. *Three—*" He holds three fingers up, like she wouldn't know what it meant without a visual representation. Condescending dick. "—large waffle fries with as much fry sauce as you can legally give me. And whatever he wants." He points at me casually, leaning his back into the booth cushion.

Seemingly intrigued, yet simultaneously concerned, the waitress turns to me, the tip of her pen hovering over her notepad.

I stare at her blankly for a minute, trying my hardest to process why Marcus is ordering mountains of fries instead of apologizing.

"Just lemon water for me, please. Thanks."

She nods, taking the menu from the table, and disappearing into the kitchen.

"Oh come on, Kane. It's Rita's. You're really not going to eat anything?"

Heat rises to the tips of my ears, and my molars make an unpleasant sound as they scrape together, my jaw tensing.

"I'm not hungry."

Marcus' brows furrow. "But... it's *Rita's.*"

Dear Universe,

Please give me the patience
not to flip my shit in my fa-
vorite local diner.

Amen

I take a very slow breath, letting the air settle in the bottom of my lungs before finally exhaling.

"I didn't come here to eat, Marcus."

A nervous laugh escapes him, his gentle white teeth shining in the low lights. "Well, yes, I know that, but—"

I don't know if it's his casualness about the situation, the feel of his body so close to mine, or the slight tug at the corner of his mouth as he looks at me. But whatever it is, causes something inside me to snap. I pull myself out of the booth, standing up quickly and running my hands through my hair.

"God I'm an idiot." I laugh humorlessly. "I mean *really*. I *actually* thought you were going to apologize. Like you even have the ability to feel remorse. Like you have the self-awareness to know when you've done something wrong. You know the sad part? *I* was going to apologize to *you*. I was fully ready to accept responsibility for the part that I played in everything. But you don't deserve that if you can't see the trainwreck that you made." A heavy stream of air pushes from my lungs, and I take one last look at his face before turning toward the door.

"Wait!" A set of thick, long fingers wrap around my arm, gently pulling me back. I rip myself from Marcus' grip, whipping around with every intention of berating him. But he doesn't give me the chance before he continues to speak. "I was going to apologize."

I settle an unconvinced gaze onto him.

"I was!" he defends. "I was getting there, I promise. I just—" His eyes drift up to meet my gaze, and I hate myself for allowing them to. "I didn't want to apologize without knowing the person I'm apologizing to."

I look at the floor, the heat in my ears expanding to my cheeks.

"You're apologizing to the person you knew," I spit.

"Yes," he replies softly. "But the person you are today deserves an apology too. I fucked up, Kane. I would take it all back if I could."

The desperation in his voice is almost convincing, until I look into his eyes and realize that it's convincing, because it's genuine. I didn't know Marcus possessed the ability to be genuine anymore. But there's this tell he has, something in his eyes that gives away his lies. His pupils recede, dullness glazes over those icy blue irises.

But that tell is nonexistent right now. And I hate that it isn't there.

years down the road
when manus are restored
and leather has worn to wood
i will thank the stars for keeping us together

-MF

Chapter Eight

MARCUS

"And here's those fries for ya!"

The young waitress sets the last basket of waffle fries in between Kane and I. He stares down at his lap, and I give her an appreciative smile.

"Thank you."

The waitress nods, wiping her palms down the front of her apron before turning and walking away. As I stare at the mountain of food in front of me, my appetite shrinks. I don't know what I was thinking; inviting Kane here, trying to reconcile things.

It's selfish, really, to think I deserve to be reconciled with. To believe that I am worthy of a second of Kane Ramirez' thoughts.

The idea eats away at me as the food on the table remains untouched.

"I'm sorry," I say, finally breaking the silence. "I shouldn't have invited you here."

Kane looks up from the floor, his amber eyes framed by thick brows, weaved together.

"Why did you?" he asks. Not harshly, nor vindictively. Softly. Curiously.

I swallow back the ache forming in the base of my throat, but my voice still cracks as I begin to speak.

"I was going to apologize," I say again. "Genuinely, and truly, with every fiber of my soul. But—" My eyes find his, and I watch as he sucks his bottom lip into his mouth, chewing on it gently.

It's a classic sign that Kane is nervous. He did it the first time we spoke. The first time I kissed him. The first time I touched him. But I have no idea why he is doing it now.

Kane terrifies me, because he is unforgettable. Of all the days I have lived, I remember the ones with him most vividly. I can't recall what I did last spring, or what I got Janelle for Christmas. But that summer repeats daily in my mind, like a tracklist you just can't let go of, always playing in the background of my life

Why he would find any bit of my existence nerve-inducing confounds me. I am extremely and entirely forgettable.

"I didn't just want to say that I was sorry. Sorry doesn't— it doesn't mean shit. Not after all this time, I know that. I don't expect forgiveness. I don't forgive myself. I don't even expect you to listen to a single word I say, but I hope that you will. Because I need you to know that you didn't deserve that. You did not deserve *any* of it."

Kane's chest jolts as his breath shudders. His bottom lip slowly slips from between his teeth, appearing glossy in the dim restaurant lighting. His eyes do too, and for a moment, I think he may cry. My stomach sinks, and I prepare myself to grab his phone and call Clara, repent for my sins, and book the first flight home. But to my surprise, he simply slides his hand across the table, picks up a waffle fry from one of the baskets between us, and pops it into his mouth.

"What?" he asks, his brow quirked and the corner of his lip turned upwards. "Sorry, I didn't listen to a single word you said."

I can't tell if he's fucking with me. I feel like, any second now, he's going to dump all the food into my lap, and storm out of the diner. The sad part is, I wouldn't blame him. But Kane continues to stare at me, with those sweet brown eyes I've always missed, and pushes one of the baskets across the table.

I finally allow myself to breathe when the little uptick of his lips breaks into a full, bright-eyed smile. Laughter swells in the bottom of his stomach until it travels up his chest, and bursts out like a cluster of bubbles, popping as he tries to catch his breath. I don't know what I did to deserve this sound, but I need to figure it out, because I might die if I never hear it again.

"Oh fuck off," I chuckle nervously, running a hand down the stubble of my beard.

"Look, Marcus. I appreciate the apology. Everything that happened back then, well... it was a long time ago. And I made mistakes too. As bizarre as this all is—" He continues laughing quietly. "It does not warrant wasting three baskets of Rita's waffle fries."

I stare at him, my brows raised.

"Are you going to eat, or just sit there catching flies with your mouth?" he asks snarkily. A confused smile breaks across my face as I comply, reaching for a perfectly golden, and crispy cross-cut fry.

There's a lot of things you forget about your hometown when you've spent such a long time away from it. How the air smells, the way the locals talk, which turn gets you to the good spot on the beach. But even if I were to wake up with amnesia, I could never forget Rita's waffle fries.

"Oh my god," I moan, tossing my head back with no dramatization. These fries are just that damn good. "They're better than I even remembered."

Kane beams proudly, the lines next to his eyes like sunrays, bringing in the light. "You're welcome."

"You're welcome?"

His brows instantly furrow. "Do I need to remind you who introduced you to those fries?"

I shove another one into my mouth, shaking my head. "Thank you."

As the clock ticks, and the baskets of fries shrink to two, then to one, I don't find myself succumbing to my regular, tireless routine. Normally, I would be in bed by now, my glasses rested on the table beside me as I drift off, ready to repeat the day tomorrow. But Kane is here, after twenty years of silence, teasing me about how boneheaded I was back then. And if I were to go to bed, I'm scared I might find that I've been dreaming all along.

Not just because Kane is talking to me; that's not entirely unbelievable. But because he is here, alive, and smiling like he means it.

Profound sadness takes a physical form in the body of Kane Ramirez. It always has, from the dark moons beneath his gorgeous brown eyes, to the gentle way his fingertips touch. How the hair on his face often needs trimmed, and the hair on his head often needs washed. From his breath, and his frown, and the little crease settled between his brows. From the pit in the stomach of everyone who's loved him, fearing that one day, he may forget it.

A beautiful devastation, and devastatingly beautiful.

"I mean, really Marcus. You brought a wet dog into a store full of books, and expected a *job?*" Lines frame his innocent smile, the reflection of the lights illuminating the golden flecks in his eyes.

"I got the job, didn't I?"

He rolls his eyes, but the smile doesn't leave his face. And for some, inexplicable reason, I'm tempted to reach out and trace it.

"I'm so sorry for interrupting," the waitress says as she approaches our table. "But we have to close early tonight. I'm sorry for any inconvenience, and am happy to box up any leftovers you wish to take." Her gaze falls to the ravished table, all but three, slightly burned fries completely demolished. I glance at Kane, his smile faltering, and then, without even realizing, I stand up.

"I should get going anyway," I say, pulling my wallet from my pocket. I hand her a fifty-dollar-bill, refusing to let my gaze drift back to Kane. "Thank you, for everything. You can keep the change."

The young woman smiles, taking the money from my hand. She looks familiar, somehow, yet I know I've never met her.

"Have a wonderful night, you two."

My eyes stay connected to her as she makes her way to the kitchen. I don't know if it's the stress of the evening, the fact that I'm not yet ready to part with Kane, or something else entirely. But I can't take my eyes off of her until she completely disappears.

From behind me, Kane clears his throat, and I fail to fight the turn of my head to look at him.

This is it. The last time I will ever see, or speak to him. The last time we'll share a meal, and a laugh. The last time I'll see the creases around his eyes, and the dimple in his cheek. The last time I will ever hear his voice.

I feel like I have so much to say, but Kane doesn't deserve that. He deserves closure. And I will do whatever I need to in order to give him that. Even if it means infinite silence.

He clears his throat again. "Do you want to walk to Sully's with me?"

i hate the sunlight
because we have to hide
and sometimes, when someone mentions
how sunny it is, i close my eyes
and wonder what could be better
than endless nights with you

—MF

Chapter Nine

KANE

I wish I could tell you that I have no idea what possessed me to ask Marcus Shane Fraund to take a walk along the beach with me. I'm pleading for my brain to come up with a single valid excuse. But the only reason sitting at the very front of my mind is loud, and clear, and obnoxious.

I missed him.

I thought, once I got my apology, that would be it. I thought it was what I needed to move on, to never think about Marcus again. But after he apologized, I still found myself wanting to stay. When he stood up to leave, I couldn't fight the infuriating urge to follow him around like a fucking dog, wondering where he was going. Wondering if I could come too. I don't know if it's nostalgia, or just the fact that sitting there with him in the diner made me feel like I wasn't alone. But whatever caused it, the feeling that "goodbye" was too soon, terrifies me entirely.

White, powdered sand funnels in the space between my feet and my sandals. I stop, sliding them off and bending down to pick them up. But as I do, my foot sinks into the soft sand, and I begin to tip sideways.

"Woah there." Marcus grabs my bicep to steady me, and my heart flutters as his fingertips tighten around me. Those soft, ridged pads, feel just as they used to. Images flash in my mind, ones of those very fingers, playing against my skin like a piano. The pictures cause blood to rush to my cheeks, and the muscle between my legs to harden slightly. Once I gain my footing, I clear my throat, and Marcus promptly lets go.

"So, Oregon State, huh? Was it everything you dreamed of?" he asks, shifting the focus. At first, I'm confused. My head whips to look at him, my brows furrowed and my chin tilted. I didn't go to Oregon State. But then I remember our conversation at Well Written, and my lie comes back to bite me in the ass.

"Yeah," I lie. "It was..." I stop, contemplating my answer. And for some reason, no matter how much I want Marcus to believe that I, too, accomplished my dreams, I cannot bring myself to continue the bluff. I don't owe Marcus shit, I know that. But I want him to know who I am. Who I *really* am. Not the person I thought I would be, and not the version he invented in his mind throughout the years, but *me*. Entirely.

"It was a lie," I admit finally. "I didn't go to Oregon State. I didn't even finish Pillar Reef."

Marcus stops walking, his feet parked just a few inches beside my own. He turns, his tall, slender body towering over me. Those crystal blue eyes lock onto mine, and the smell of his vanilla-bourbon cologne is potent and delectable. Sculpted, grey brows knit together, and I can't bear the thought of seeing the disappointment about to fill his face, so I look away.

"Why lie about it?" he asks quietly. I swallow back an aching lump forming in the base of my throat.

"I—" A shaky breath slips from my lips. "I wanted you to think I was successful. Like you."

Silence creeps into the vacancy between us, and I stare shamefully down at the sand. My stomach twists into a knot that tightens every time I inhale. Then, a burst of humorless laughter pierces the silence.

"You think I'm *successful*?" Marcus scoffs, clutching his stomach. A glossy coat forms over his eyes as he continues to chuckle uncontrollably.

I frown. "You're a full-time, award winning author."

Still laughing, Marcus shakes his head. "Sure," he says. "If that's what you call success."

"I mean, what else could you want, Marc?"

His laughter begins to die down, and he looks at me curiously. "If you didn't go to Oregon State, what were you up to all those years?"

My lips part, and I want so badly to tell him off. To ask him how that's relevant, and to scold him for laughing at me. But instead, I just answer honestly.

"Nothing. I continued to work at Well Written, and when Old Man Duke passed, I took it over. Clara and I also got married, which *dearly* went well."

Shame creeps over me as heat begins to flood my cheeks. Here is Marcus, accomplished and handsome and successful. And I have done nothing except divorce my best friend.

"Wait, you and Clara got *married*?" His brows shoot up, and I swear his eyes bulge out of his head. I chuckle, still embarrassed.

"Yeah, like I said, that ended well." I shake my head. "It was dumb. I was sad, and she was lonely, and we were best friends. It was a pact, kind of."

Marcus looks at the horizon, the setting sun casting a golden glow across his chiseled cheeks. He sighs.

"Do you regret it?" he asks.

It's not a new question, as I've asked it myself many times. I don't have to hesitate with my answer.

"If I didn't, she probably wouldn't have met Derrick. And in turn, Judah wouldn't have been born, so—" I shake my head again, and a soft smile creeps across my face. "No."

Marcus smiles too, shallow lines forming around his upturned lips. The sunset creates a radiant reflection in his blue eyes, making them sparkle like the ocean waves beside us. It seems, despite the years that have passed, his eyes are aging backwards, because there's a bright glow in them that was never there before. Sure, he's got crows feet and worry lines. But something about him feels more youthful than he seemed at twenty-two.

"Then it wasn't stupid," he says, beginning to walk again.

I follow quickly beside him, a question dancing anxiously on the tip of my tongue. I shouldn't care. I don't care, really. I'm just curious, is all. Anxiously curious. "Well, what about you? Did you get married?"

Marcus stares straight ahead, his throat bobbing as he swallows. "Never found the right person." His hand runs through his hair, and he quickly changes the subject. "Do you know why I don't consider myself successful, Kane?"

"Because you can always be better?" I ask sarcastically. Marcus was always focused on how he could improve. In school, in writing, at work, with his parents. He was never content with himself, so it's no surprise he feels the same about his career.

But Marcus shakes his head. "Because I'm *alone*, Kane. Completely and utterly alone. You got divorced, sure, but look at all the people in your life who care about you. Judah, Clara, her *husband,* for fucks sake. I mean, who likes their wife's ex? But he does. He *loves* you. And that's—" His voice cracks, but he doesn't allow me to get a good look at his face as he walks. "*That's* success, right there. Because all of this, everything I have, it's superficial. When you're having a hard time, or you're feeling alone, what do you do?"

I don't realize he actually intends me to answer until he turns, and looks down at me. And even with the vermillion sun shining in my eyes, I can see a single tear trickling down his cheek. My throat begins to tighten as I answer.

"I go to Clara's," I say quietly. Marcus smiles.

"Do you know what I do?" he asks, turning to look ahead again. "I write. I create fictional characters to be there for me, because I pushed everyone I've ever cared about, out of my life. So if you want to call my career success? That's fine. But just know that what you have, that family you've created out of care, and love, and sadness, is infinitely more valuable than any award I will ever win. I'm not the victor in all of this, Kane. I haven't *won* anything. And I'm not looking for pity. I don't want you, or *anyone*, to feel sorry for me. I did this to myself. But I just want you to know that what I did, leaving everyone like that instead of facing it all, it was the biggest mistake of my life. And no amount of book deals or bestseller lists will ever change that."

Marcus isn't trying to guilt me. He's hurt me, and left me, but he has never intentionally made me feel like I did something wrong.

But as I stand here with him, listening to painful words pour out of his pretty lips, I can't help but feel like it's all my fault. It doesn't make sense. He's the one who turned on me, the one who left. Still, that doesn't stop my stomach from turning into an immovable mass.

It doesn't stop the memories of that summer from coming back to me, all the fights, all the pressure I put on him.

My chest begins to sink as I recount those nights, nausea washing over me in waves much stronger than the ones we walk beside.

"It was so fucked up," I cry, pinching the bridge of my nose between my thumb and index finger to fight back tears. "I should have never expected you to come out before you were ready. I should have let it go. I should've—"

Marcus grabs my shoulder, shaking his head.

"No, Kane. Don't say that. *Please,* please don't say that. You didn't do anything wrong. I was a coward. It was unfair of me to expect you to keep us a secret. You were proud of who you were. You always have been. And I am so fucking envious of that."

I swallow, an tight sensation tugging at my vocal chords as I take in his words. I have always been proud of who I am, but I was raised to be. Marcus wasn't awarded the same luxury. He was a victim of circumstance, and I might not forgive him for leaving, but I can still mourn his youth.

"You were right to be scared. I mean, look at your parents! Look how they reacted. I—" I sigh, shaking my head. "I just didn't want to feel like I was creeping back into the closet, Marcus. I *couldn't* go back."

Marcus' hand settles deeper into my shoulder, his smooth palm nesting itself into the crook of my neck. He looks at me, earnestly, and doesn't speak until I finally meet his gaze.

"Kane, the one and *only* reason that I have nobody in my life, is because I chose to run from them all. I ran from you, I ran from my parents, and I ran from myself. There is *nothing* you could have done to prevent that. No matter how supportive you were, I was never going to be ready to accept myself back then."

I don't know how to respond to Marcus, because it's not like I can tell him that he's wrong. Looking back at that summer, I can't picture him ever coming out on his own accord, no matter how many times I dreamed of it. It's tragic, really, to hate yourself before ever really knowing who you are.

I understand it completely.

"Can I ask you something?" he inquires quietly. The wind picks up, causing the waves to crash harder onto the shore. Salty ocean water sprays us gently, and I nod, wiping my cheek onto my shoulder. "How have you been? Like, actually?"

I try not to look directly at him, but his presence is magnetic, and I catch myself staring anyway. I scan his eyes, searching for genuineness in his question. His bright gaze doesn't back down.

"Okay," I answer quietly. But when his eyes lock back onto mine, I can tell he doesn't believe me. "It's been bad, lately. But I'm working on it."

"When did that start?" he asks.

"What?"

"You haven't always wanted to work on it," he explains truthfully. "So when did you start wanting to?"

My breath hitches, and I have no time, nor the energy, to come up with an elaborate lie. So I don't. I look at him earnestly, and I tell him the unaltered truth.

"Do you remember that night we went to the lighthouse to look at constellations?" I ask. He nods.

"That was the night before—" His voice catches, and I continue for him.

"Yes, the night before you left. That night, you told me that it felt like life was invented specifically for us."

His brows weave together, and he sucks his cheeks in nervously. "Yeah?"

"I decided to *pretend* you were right. To start acting like life was created specifically for me to enjoy it. To take advantage of the world around me, and soak in every rain drop, and interaction, and accident. I know it's dumb. Selfish, even. But it's like you said. 'When someone gives you a gift, it's rude to never touch it.'"

God, it's stupid. Humiliating, even, that I've held onto that piece of him for so long. And it's even worse that I've just admitted it out loud.

But I flinch as Marcus brushes a strand of hair out of my eyes, and says:

"You've come a long way, Kane. You know that?"

An awkward laugh slips out of me, and I scratch the back of my neck nervously.

"I don't know. Is it really a long way if I still feel the same?"

Marcus' feet stop moving, planting themselves directly in front of mine. His hands wrap around the back of each of my biceps, and his eyes look into mine intently.

"You're still here," he says. "And you're still trying. So yes, Kane. You've come a long fucking way."

"Welcome to Sully's! What can I get started for you?" The employee smacks his gloved hands together, shooting us a very plastic grin. I glance at Marc, but he isn't even looking at the menu. His arms are crossed over his chest like he knows exactly what he wants. Like he came prepared.

Then, a memory floods into my brain. It takes up each corner of my mind, playing in front of my eyes like a scene from a movie.

We're here, in the same exact spot we are now, only younger. Marc is shoveling a spoonful of pink ice into my mouth, and the second it melts onto my tongue, I cringe, spitting it out onto the white sand beneath us.

"What the fuck was that?!" I asked with disgust. My nose wrinkled, and I kept gagging and coughing, trying to get the heinous flavor off of my tongue.

Marc laughed brightly, the corners of his lips turned upwards.

"Hibiscus."

I spat onto the sand again. "Well it's disgusting."

Marcus' smile transitioned into a subtle smirk, the lines next to his mouth deepening.

"I like it."

"You would."

"Why, because it's gross?"

I rolled my eyes. "No, because if you were a flower, you'd totally be a hibiscus."

Marcus' gaze turned confused, his brows furrowing together. "And why's that?"

"I'd rather not say."

His brow twitched, and a coy smile tugged on the corner of his lip. "Well, you'd be a rose," he said, taking another heaping bite. I shot him an unamused glance.

"Why, because of the thorns?"

An irritatingly sweet smile crept across his face.

"Bingo."

My focus shifts back to Marcus, his finger pointing at the pink syrup behind the counter.

"Can I get a hibiscus snow cone please?" he asks, and when he turns to look at me, the slight upturn of his lips makes me wonder if the same memory popped into his brain.

I consider making a joke about it. Telling him that hibiscus snow cones are an "abomination", and a "threat to society". But Marcus looks back to the employee behind the stand, and I realize that I was foolish to think he'd ever remember a moment so insignificant.

"And for you, sir?" the teenage boy asks. I swallow back the lump forming in my throat, and scramble in my brain to think of a single flavor that isn't the wretched, nauseating "hibiscus". But nothing comes to mind. I just keep seeing him, Marc, twenty years younger, that stupid smirk plastered on his face.

"He'll take a hibiscus as well," I hear Marc answer. My eyes race to meet his in a horrified gaze, and I'm just about to wave down the Sully's employee and beg him to not give me a hibiscus fucking snow cone, when my eye catches on the little crescent settled into the side of Marc's mouth. It's subtle, and nostalgic, and teasing. And I realize that Marcus, is fucking with me.

Laughter bursts out of him like a flame, and he clutches his side, taking in staggered breaths.

"You should see your face!" He wipes a tear from his eye, then doubles back over, letting out a sound that nearly resembles a howl.

I want to frown, I really do. I want to silently display how unamusing I found that little prank, and inform Marc of the uproar that would ensue if I was, in fact, delivered a hibiscus snow cone.

But I can't.

Because Marcus remembered that night, and now, it's all I'll be able to think about.

"I'll take a pina colada, actually," I answer, failing to fight the smile stretched across my lips. The employee, completely unaware, and un-interested of the history behind Marc's laughter, promptly nods, and begins forming the shaved ice.

The wind is fierce tonight. Heavy gushes of air blow against Marcus and I, causing both of us to shiver as we walk along the beach. But that doesn't stop us from continuing to shovel cold, flavored ice shavings into our mouth as we bury our feet in the sand.

"Fuck!" Marcus holds his jaw open, breathing heavily through his mouth and wincing.

"Brain freeze?" I ask, and he nods quickly.

"Sho' col'," he manages to get out, still exhaling warm air to soothe the freezing sensation. Even with his jaw awkwardly hanging open, Marcus looks regal and handsome.

I love the way the shirt he's wearing fits him, and how the color is reminiscent to his eyes. I love how he leaves the top button open, his smooth, hairless chest peeking from beneath. And the way it hugs his arms, like they just barely fit into the sleeves. I love the way his pants sit on his waist, and how they're ever so slightly tight around his hips. It's flattering, to say the least. And I'm just now realizing that I'm staring.

"Do you want to try mine?" I ask, hoping the gesture disguises my gaze. I hold out a little red spoon piled with a mountain of shaved ice. Marcus nods, shakes his head, then nods again.

"I do," he says in his normal voice. The brain freeze must be fading. "But I need to give my brain a break for a second."

"Slow was never your forte," I tease, scooping the bite into my mouth. Heat begins to rush to my cheeks as I realize the suggestiveness of my comment, but it only takes a moment for a different sensation to take over. A freezing, throbbing pain shoots from the roof of my mouth, into every fold of my brain. My head tosses back, and now, I take my turn to mouth-breathe.

Marcus erupts into a ball of low, rumbling laughter. It feels like thunder when the sun is still shining. Deep, and full, but still bright and safe. One thing that hasn't changed about Marcus is his laugh, and I'm more grateful for that than I'd like to admit.

"Clearly, it wasn't yours either," he taunts, and I'd roll my eyes if it didn't feel like I was trapped in an agonizing ice-coffin.

Once my brain begins to thaw, and my clenched eyes open, I realize that Marcus is standing perpendicular to me. His body is nestled close to mine, his arms hovered around my body like a contactless cocoon.

"What are you doing?" I ask annoyedly, taking a step away from him. Marcus waves his hands, gesturing for me to come back to him.

"Protecting you!" he yells back as the wind picks up. I almost pull even further away, but Marcus looks so worried right now, and I have to admit that it's rather cute. I battle the wind as I shuffle closer to him. Not close enough to touch, but just enough to where I can feel the heat radiating from his body.

"We should go back!" I suggest, my voice barely carrying through the thick air. Marc shakes his head.

"It's too far!" He points at a silhouette in the distance, and as I squint my eyes, the shape becomes clear. "The lighthouse is the closest option!"

I consider arguing, but as the thought enters my brain, little flecks of sand begin to pelt my legs and cheeks, and I accept the very plain fact that I would rather be trapped in a lighthouse with Marcus, than endure another second of this whipping, stinging sensation.

My eyes lock onto his, and the moment Marc gives me a singular nod, we both begin to run to the lighthouse.

My vision becomes blurry as the wind picks up the sand around us, transforming it's usual clarity into visible puffs of sediment. It feels like someone is slicing a thousand papercuts into the sides of my legs, and as we approach the door, Marcus grabs the rusted handle, and swings it open. It creaks eerily as it closes behind us, and a loud, metallic echo rings through the building.

Then, silence.

If I am a flower

Then you are a bee

I only exist

Because of your kiss

-MF

Chapter Ten

MARCUS

The lighthouse feels drastically more haunted than she did the last time I stepped inside. Nothing looks inherently different, but something feels off. *Vacant.*

It's stupid, I know, because this lighthouse was empty long before Kane and I ever stepped inside. But she feels even more abandoned now, and I wonder if we are the first visitors she's had since the last time we entered.

"Do you remember her being this... creepy?" Kane asks, his brows knitted together.

I can't help but let out a soft chuckle as I look at him. His thick, brown hair is pushed to one side from the wind, and his warm eyes are round and worried.

Kane used to tease me about my belief that Roberta, the lighthouse, was haunted by her old keeper. But from the furrow of his brow, and the slight downturn of his lips, I think, after twenty years, he is finally beginning to believe me.

"Roberta has come for revenge," I taunt, and the whites of Kane's eyes grow even wider.

"Don't say that!" He waves his hands in the air like it will rid us of the ghosts inhabiting the space. "That's not funny, Marc."

I point at a rusted blue barrel against the wall, and approach it, tossing in the remnants of my snow cone. Kane follows, casting his garbage on top of mine. I peek through the window at the sea, watching as giant waves crash into the shore.

"We might be stuck here for awhile," I say hesitantly. Kane's dissatisfaction only intensifies, and he quickly squeezes his body beside mine, peering through the window to confirm my assessment.

A loud sigh comes from the depths of his chest, which I can only assume means that he reluctantly agrees. Something needs to fill the silence that follows. Not because it's awkward with Kane, but because it isn't. Because it feels so instinctive, so right to just stand here saying nothing, even after all this time. And I'm afraid of what I might do if things continue to feel so natural.

"So..." I pause, trying to find something, anything, to fill this comfortable void. "Why didn't you leave? After dinner, I mean."

Jesus. If Kane wasn't watching me with a deer-in-the-headlights type of stare, I would be palming my sweating forehead out of embarrassment. Asking him why he decided to stay with me, while he has no option to leave, is a truly terrible question. But, at the very least, it adds some much-needed discomfort to the situation.

Kane's wide eyes blink slowly at me, and he clears his throat.

"I uh—" He swallows, the knot on his jugular bouncing. "Well, I wanted to ask you about your writing."

"Oh, right," I nod, clicking my tongue to the roof of my mouth. I don't know why that sentence made my stomach sink. Maybe because I'm so used to people only wanting to be around me for the art that

I create, or maybe because I was secretly hoping, that maybe, just maybe, Kane asked me to walk with him, because he missed me too.

It's ridiculous, I know, but I can't stop wondering anyway. I never have been able to get it off my mind, what things would have been like if I hadn't left.

Would we have moved in together? Gotten married? Would Kane have ever decided to try living?

It's all pointless to think about, because in the end, I never would have accepted myself the way I needed to for him to be happy. For that to happen, I had to escape. But I think about it anyway, and sometimes, I wonder what would have happened if he had simply come with me.

"What do you want to ask me?"

Kane's gaze drops to the floor, and he chews nervously on the inside of his cheek. "It's dumb, actually. I don't know why—"

"It's not dumb."

He looks up at me, those russet brown eyes soft, and warm, and nervous. A shaky breath slips from his mouth.

"Well, I- I wanted to know. *Harrison's Affair*?"

My gut tightens as the words leave his mouth, and I know there is no real way out of this conversation. This *confession*.

"Yeah?"

"I just wondered if— well, if—" Kane seems to be having trouble getting his words out, and the intelligent thing to do would be to let him stutter and fluster until he decides to give up on the question. But Kane deserves the truth, and I will never give him less than he deserves again.

"It's about you," I confirm quietly. "*Us*."

Kane's expression shifts into something unrecognizable, and when he speaks, his voice sounds hoarse and choked.

"Why?"

I know I need to answer him. I know he needs to understand. But it's hard, to admit out loud, that I never really stopped loving Kane.

"I wanted to see a reality where I never left." After I say it, I realize that the lighthouse was never silent until now. I can't hear anything. Not the wind, not the ocean, not Kane's breath. "I'm sorry. I shouldn't have said that."

He shakes his head, clearing his throat.

"No, I asked."

Quiet looms in every square foot of this place. Even the whistle of the air outside has been completely drown out by the heavy pulse filling my ear drums. The last time we were here, was the last time I saw Kane before I left, and I think that fact is weighing heavy on the both of us.

"So, *Heartless Heights*. What inspired that one?" he asks suddenly. I break into a soft, sad chuckle. He was never good at being subtle. I loved that about him. *Love.* I love that about him.

"Did you like it?" I ask, allowing him to divert the conversation. It's a courtesy to the both of us, even if I could, in theory, talk about Harrison's Affair all day. And judging by the annotations and erosion of his copy, Kane could too.

He pauses, looking to the top of the stairs. "I have to admit," he finally answers. "It wasn't my favorite of yours."

It feels like I've swallowed the sun. Hot, beaming energy filling my stomach when Kane speaks. Part of it is his voice, sure. It's raspy, and soothing and timid. But it's the words that come from his mouth that mean the most to me, because I have never been understood in the way Kane understands me.

"I'm glad you said that," I reply, running my hand along my jaw. "Because I fucking hate that one."

Immediately, Kane frowns, pressing his brows together. "*What? Why?*"

"You tell me." I smile. Kane looks defensive, and nervous, like he's scared to hurt my feelings. That's another thing I've always loved about him. As honest as he may be, Kane is always kind.

"I didn't say I hate it. I said it wasn't my favorite of yours," he clarifies.

I roll my eyes. "C'mon, Kane. Be mean for once in your life. Tell me what you really think."

"I don't want to."

The way he looks at me, how the sunset reflects off the lighter shades of brown in his eyes, makes me want to back down, and give him what he wants. *Anything* he wants, always. It's hard to understand how long you can be apart from someone, and still, some things never change.

"Alright," he says defeatedly. Then, he straightens his posture, holding his head high. "I can be mean."

"Sure." I smile. "Go ahead."

waves retreat the same way as i
but when the water begins
to creep back to the shore
know that i am there too
making my way back to you
-MF

Chapter Eleven

KANE

Marcus is staring at me like it's a challenge.

I don't like it.

Or, maybe I do like it, but I hate that I like it? I hate how it reminds me of that summer. I hate that it causes my chest to swell with heat, and my heart to pound heavier against my ribcage. I hate the betraying stiffening forming between my legs. But most of all, I hate that he thinks he still knows me, and I hate that he might not be wrong.

"I didn't like *Heartless Heights* because—" I take a deep breath. Marcus likes the truth, and honesty is important to me too. But right now, I don't feel as if I'm talking to Marc. I feel like I'm talking to Carsen V. Lovett. My favorite author. And suddenly, being honest, feels extremely intimidating. "I don't like it because it felt undeveloped. Or— I don't know, maybe that isn't the right word. It felt forced?"

I flip through the pages of a mental thesaurus, trying to find the word to convey what I mean. I'm not a writer, like Marcus. I don't have a way with words. When I speak, the only thing the people around me feel is sadness. And not in a profound, tugging on your heartstrings way. More of a "this poor, pitiful dude" way.

"I guess what I'm trying to say is that it didn't feel like *you*."

I stare up at Lovett— I mean, *Marcus*— nervously. But the anxiousness turns into irritation as a loud laugh erupts from deep within his chest.

"Why are you laughing?" I ask defensively. Marcus wipes a tear from his eye, then turns away from me. His shoulders move up and down, which tells me that even though I can't hear it, he's still laughing. "What's so funny?"

He shakes his head.

"Nothing," he chuckles, turning to face me. Small wrinkles form at the corners of his eyes. "It's just— some things never change."

Something in my stomach sinks, and even though I know Marcus didn't mean anything by it, the sentence bothers me. I don't disagree with him, necessarily, but I want to. I don't want to be the same exact person I was back then. I don't want to be in the same exact place.

"I've changed," I say, but it feels like a failed attempt to convince only myself.

Marcus looks down at me, those soft blue eyes glowing with endearment. Then, he smiles.

"Only in the best ways."

My heart palpitates violently as I stare back at him. I want to ask him how he knows that, since he's barely seen me for a day. But even more, I want to ask him what that means. I want to know what he sees in me. I want to know what makes me worthy of his time.

But Marcus doesn't give me the opportunity to ask. Instead, his gaze shoots to the top of the stairs again, and a mischievous smile stretches across his face. Then, he takes off, barreling up the spiral staircase like a bolt of lightning.

Despite my confusion, I begin to race after him, not even thinking to hide my curious smile as I chase him.

"Really?" I call out, though the faux irritation is obviously so, given the laugh that follows. "Marc, that's completely unfair!"

"What's unfair?" he yells back childishly, his feet still moving. I blow out an exasperated breath, slowing down but still maintaining a running pace.

"You got a head start!"

He throws his hands up, stopping on the very last step to look down at me. His eyes shimmer as he smiles at me, his chest heaving from the impromptu cardio. As he gets closer, I notice the small droplets of sweat beading at the crown of his head, and I remember the way Marcus smells when he sweats.

It's a salty, and sweet, but also musky aroma. A scent, for some reason, I miss even more than the stray love letters and arguments about hibiscus snow cones. If they made a candle that smells like Marcus Fraund, the shelves would be empty.

When I round the final curve, Marc steps onto the main floor, and as my foot hits the top step, that sweet, nostalgic scent fills my nose. It washes over me, the hairs on my arms standing up like their reaching for it. Desperate for it.

I'm so busy soaking in the scent that I don't realize, until this moment, that I am completely and utterly winded. My chest heaves and I lean over, placing my palms on my knees as I pant heavily.

"Not as young as we used to be," Marcus chuckles breathily. I nod, continuing to gasp for air.

"Jesus Christ." I blow out a heavy breath. "Was it always that long?"

He smirks. "Were you always that slow?"

I shove an elbow playfully into his side, and Marcus chuckles, running a hand through his hair.

I love the way it flows, a mesmerizing grey gradient. It's adorable, and I wonder if it still feels as soft as it used to. If it smells like the product he always used.

"Look," Marcus points through the window, at the sun setting over the sea. It causes the ocean to glow a deep orange color, and makes the clouds blush. He reaches for the door to the balcony, and pushes it open.

As we step outside, the wind funnels into my ears. I look to Marc, his styled hair blowing into a greying mess on the top of his head. I like seeing Marcus messy and imperfect, because I know how much he hates it. It was all he ever thought about back then; pleasing the people around him. That was the only good thing about him leaving. I knew he wasn't going to run off and go to law school, like his parents always wanted. He was going to write.

And he did.

"It's cold!" Marcus shouts over the wind. I smile at him, and nod, but neither of us moves. "Has it always been this beautiful?"

My head turns to look up at him, but he continues to stare out at the scarlet ocean. His jaw is square and pronounced, his lips curved and pale. And as I watch him admire the view in front of us, I realize that he might not be so different from the man I loved back then. The only thing that's changed, is that now, he loves himself too.

It's a dangerous realization, because if that's what stopped us before, what's going to stop us right now?

"It has been," I answer. But what I'm taking in before my very eyes is infinitely more beautiful than the ocean view. Marcus places his hand onto the railing, right next to mine. The side of his palm touches me, but I don't pull away, even though I know I should. In fact, I do the complete opposite. My hand slowly creeps closer, my fingers carefully intertwining with his. His skin is soft, and warm, and the pulsing, tensing sensation between my thighs returns. Marcus' jaw tenses, but he doesn't pull away either.

"I think about it too, sometimes," I say, before I even have the chance to process it. "About what would have happened if you stayed."

Marcus looks at me, and though his mouth doesn't budge, something in his eyes makes it feel as though he smiling.

"Yeah?" he asks, so quietly that I have to read his lips. I nod.

"Yeah."

"And?"

My chest tightens, and I fix my gaze back onto the ocean. "I don't know," I admit. "I think you would have continued to please your parents. You would have given up writing, and gone to law school, and there wouldn't have been any room for me in that life."

My throat bobs as I swallow, and out of the corner of my eye, I can see Marcus' chin tilting down, his gaze moving to his feet.

"You're probably right," he says. His hand turns over so that his palm is rested against mine. Then, his fingers slide into the spaces between mine, and he tugs me gently so that my body is against his. I feel his warm breath against the top of my head. I smell his sweet, musky aroma filling the air around us. My heart begins to thrum violently in my chest, and before I even know what I'm doing, I look up at him, cupping his cheek with my spare hand.

"What about this life?" I ask. Then, I push myself onto the tips of my toes, and press my lips against his.

a beacon dances over the waves
the lighthouse, your lips,
guiding me home

-MF

Chapter Twelve

MARCUS

The taste of pineapple and coconut on Kane's lips has fainted, and all I taste is him. It's everything I wanted, everything I remembered. As my tongue slides gently between his teeth, it traces that small scar against the inside of his cheek. It feels just as it did all those years ago. Deep, and ridged. Permanent.

"Marcus," he groans desperately, tugging at the collar of my shirt. I don't know what to do with his plea. On one hand, I know how this will end. I'm well aware that the dent inside his cheek isn't his only scar. That should be enough for me to stop this. Enough to remind me that all I do is disappoint people. Hurt them. But I can't stop myself from pulling Kane further into my body. From praying I'll get to desperately devour every inch of him.

"Kane," I mumble, running my hands through his hair. It's so thick, and so grabbable, but I don't have the urge to twirl it around my fingers and pull. I want to touch him gently. Carefully. *Lovingly*. Like I've missed doing for all these years. My fingers slide down the softness of his stomach until they reach the hem of his shirt. They journey underneath the fabric, grazing the coarse hairs around his navel. I want him desperately. All of him.

"This is a bad idea," he groans, his head falling back as my lips attach to the sensitive spot along the underside of his jaw. I pull back slightly, letting my breath hover over the area I've bruised.

Fuck.

It's like I'm a teenager all over again.

"Do you want to stop?" I ask, the wind around us picking up. Kane shakes his head.

"No," he answers, his finger tracing the outline of my jaw. But as I go to press myself back against him, I'm greeted with outstretched hands. "I'm sorry, Marc. I really am. I didn't mean to— I just can't do this."

Kane steps back, tears welling in his eyes, and he takes one last shaky breath before pulling the balcony door open, and quickly disappearing inside.

Time is a fickle beast. When you want it to stop, everything transforms into an unmemorable blur. And when all you desire is that blur, so that you can move on to the next point, it decides to move so slowly, you feel as if you're frozen. Stuck in one place, every minute a growing torture.

I roll over to peer at the clock on the bedside table.

3:07

"Jesus," I groan, running my hand down my face. I've been laying here, staring at the ceiling for *five hours*. Only, it hasn't felt like I've been staring at the ceiling. I've been picturing Kane the entire time. His dimpled smile, his desperate pleas. His shuddered breath, and those beautiful brown eyes looking up at me. I shouldn't have let it happen, I know that. But it's hard to deny yourself something you want so desperately. And now, I'm laying in bed, wondering if Kane, too, is staring at his ceiling.

I wonder if he's thinking of me. I wonder if he's regretting it all.

I fumble around for my glasses, blindly feeling the thin wire and thick lenses between my fingers as I put them on. Then, I pull my laptop off the nightstand, and into my lap, the screen illuminating the room as I open it.

Immediately, a blank white page stares back at me, the cursor blinking in a steady rhythm. Lately, I've been finding it taunting. A repetitive reminder of how empty my mind has been lately. Of how much I despise the project I'm working on.

Now, I find it relieving. Comforting. Every second that it blinks, words flood to the front of my mind, begging for their turn on the page. I don't know where it all came from, the ideas, the excitement. But I have a sneaking suspicion that it has to do with Kane.

I never had writer's block when I was with Kane. Every time my pencil paused, I'd look over at him, and feel inspiration. From his aura, and his eyes, and the stupid way his body moves as he laughs. Every time I thought that I was out of words, he'd give me new ones without even speaking.

My hands hover over the keyboard, and the second my fingertip touches the first letter, they all begin a fast-paced dance across my lap. Words fill the screen before I even have the chance to process what they mean. But they must mean something, because they're demanding to be said.

Sentences pour out of me in a way they haven't for years. Every few minutes, a new page is created, filled with the thoughts consuming me. It's taken me three months to write ninety words, but it's taken me four hours to write five chapters. *Long ones.*

I wonder how I could be so disconnected from this story for so long. It's such a beautiful one, full of love, and family, and ambition. It's magnificent, and sad, and it's coming to life before my dry, bloodshot eyes.

"Marcus?" A soft knock rings through the door. "Do you still want to go to La Luna?"

Fuck.

I forgot I promised Janelle we would go to the cafe this morning and work on her novel. *Novels*, actually, and though the series really is coming along great, I don't want to go. I want to see Kane, and apologize. But even more, I want to kiss him again, and tell him that there is room for him in this life, because I saved him a seat next to me all this time.

But I can't cancel on her. Nellie puts up with *everything*, all my back-and-forth, my forgetfulness, my *tardiness*, with the promise that I will help her with her goals. Well, that, and the fat paycheck. But I know which is more important to her, which is why she is going to be even more successful than I am.

"I'm coming!" I call out, watching the little circular arrow spin until I'm sure my progress has saved. I shut the laptop, and slide out of bed, quickly getting ready for the day.

La Luna is a dockside cafe, overlooking the gorgeous ocean. You can feel the waves beneath you as you dine, and while some may find that it makes it hard to focus, I experience the opposite. It's like a baby, being rocked to sleep. Except instead, it's my work, coming to life. It was my favorite place to write in college, besides Well Written of course.

"Sorry," I mumble, wiping the crust from my eyes as I open the door. Nellie's head tilts as she analyzes me, her shiny, sculpted brow lifted slightly.

"You look like shit." She smiles teasingly. "Rough night?"

I frown. "Thanks."

"I'm *kidding*, Marc," she giggles, nudging me with her elbow. "But really, did you sleep at all?"

I shake my head. "Better. I *wrote*."

With espresso running through my veins, and a half-empty bottle of eyedrops beside me, I settle further into the suede couch at the cafe.

"This is good stuff," I tell Janelle, refusing to take my eyes off the screen. Janelle writes fantasy, a genre I don't particularly partake in, neither writing nor reading. Yet, she's created something so captivating, I'm reconsidering my choices.

"Tell me what you really think," she says, glancing up from her laptop. I raise my brows at her, and a smile breaks across my face as I remember the night before. Kane, confirming that even now, he hasn't forgotten me. But this is different, of course, because Janelle's third book is everything Heartless Heights isn't. It's genius, and passionate, and captivating.

"I'm serious, Nellie. It's-" I pause, thinking of the proper verbiage. If I use the wrong words, Janelle is going to think I'm simply being kind. "It's original, but palatable. The plot is really different from the first and second books, but it works, because of the character development you've accomplished. I think— Well, I think you're ready to query."

Janelle gives me an unamused expression, her chin tilted down and her brow quirked to display just how unconvinced she is by my compliments. But when I don't laugh, or contort my face in any way, her expression slowly transforms into subtle excitement.

"Do you really think so?" she asks quietly. I nod.

"I think any agent who rejects it, is going to seriously regret their decisions when it gets turned into a movie series."

Now, Janelle can't hide her joy. She beams proudly, her cheeks glowing red and her dark eyes sparkling. She's proud of herself, and it's amazing. It's hard to be proud of yourself sometimes. Especially when the world around you is always finding reasons why you shouldn't be. But Janelle has experience in this industry. She knows what she's getting herself into.

And yet, she is proud anyway.

"How's it looking over *there?* I ask nervously, wincing as my eyes land onto her laptop. The worst part of writing at night, is waking up in the morning and deleting it all, because in your sleep-deprived delirium, you thought it was a grand idea to go completely off the rails.

I mean, what is plot if not a series of poor decisions made by the main character, right?

Her forehead wrinkles as her eyes scan the screen again, and she looks back up at me.

"It's a mess," she admits, but a sweet smile settles into the groove of her mouth. "But it's something. It's a lot of something, actually, and I can see where it's going. If you keep at this rate—" She pretends to look at an invisible watch on her wrist. "You'll have a completed novel, a *good* one, in four weeks." The pads of her index and middle fingers drag across the touchpad, the document scrolling down to reveal page after page. "Where was all of this the last three months?"

My palm runs across the back of my sweating neck.

"Oh, I don't know..." I divert, but Nellie doesn't buy my feigned oblivion.

"Oh really?" Her tone is high and taunting. "So, it has *nothing* to do with your meetup with Kane last night?"

Heat creeps across my face, and I know from the burning sensation, that my cheeks have to be some deep shade of pink. But I shake my head, pretending the facade is still in play.

"Nope."

Nellie nods skeptically. "So it's a complete coincidence that you've written nothing for three months, yet the night you happen to be with him for hours, you write a tenth of a book?"

I suck my lips inward, pinching them between my teeth. If there's one thing to know about Janelle, it's that she will always see through you. "So weird, right?"

"See you back at the hotel!" Nellie calls out from across the street. I wave at her, and watch as she disappears into a painted pink clothing shop with sales racks along the sidewalk.

Coral Beach undeniably has one of the best downtown areas I've ever been to. All the shops stare out at the ocean, the walls boasting colorful, pastel shades. And even though it's a somewhat small town, you can buy anything you'd ever want by just walking along the strip. Clothes, shoes, cell phones, food, the list is truly endless. It's not like Phoenix.

Giant shopping malls don't block the gorgeous views, and every business is small and local. I have to admit that I miss the intimacy of it. I visit the same cafe in Arizona weekly, and could only tell you one of the employee's names. But here? I used to know everyone.

Every store owner, every kid at school. Every sanitation worker, and PTA mom, and even every dog living in the town. I used to hate it. I dreamed of living somewhere new. Somewhere so big that nobody cared what I did, or who I was. I wanted to bury myself in a sea of people, so that maybe, just maybe, I wouldn't have to try as hard to hide. But now that I'm back, now that I'm here, I forgot how nice it feels to be seen. To have people smile at you as you walk past, or hold the door open. To ask you how your day was, and really truly care about your answer. You could go anywhere in Coral Beach and find that. But there's only one place I've ever felt the same acceptance at in Phoenix.

The library.

There isn't anything particularly special about the library in Phoenix. But there is something so spectacular about libraries in general, anywhere you go. They are full of many things: books, dust, weird stains in the darkly-colored carpets. But there is one thing you will never fail to find in any library:

Loving people.

And that's something I learned in this very town.

I walk along the sidewalk, looking out at the ocean as I make my way to the Coral Beach Public Library. I don't know why my feet are moving in that direction, like it's muscle memory. I can't remember deciding it was my destination, but I don't think I could turn around even if I wanted to. The library is where I've always gone when my head is spinning. Something about browsing the shelves makes the entire world around me disappear. All I can focus on is finding the right book, and completely submerging myself in it.

The only problem is this:

That solution doesn't apply to Kane. He follows me into each story, filling the role of the love interest or the best friend. Even, sometimes, the main character. Every time I've tried to escape Kane Ramirez, he ricochets back into the core of my brain, the marrow of my bones, the beat of my heart. I've been running from him for twenty years, and yet, I have been going in circles, because I've been chasing him too.

In every book I've written. In every dream I've had. Kane has been at the center of all of it, and I may not see him ever again.

As I approach the library, embellished with tall windows and vivid memories, I have to wonder *why*. Why, after all these years, would Kane and I be pulled back together, just to retreat back into our old lives at the end of it. All of this, the party, the apology, the kiss, none of it felt like closure. We were supposed to tie a thread, and yet, it seems it has merely unraveled even further. And I might not know Kane the way I used to, but I know him well enough to say that he feels the same. He has to, because otherwise, he wouldn't have kissed me like it was the middle of a sentence. Like more was to follow, like it was just the beginning.

I stare at the glass doors in front of me, my reflection staring back. But as soon as I recognize myself, it quickly begins to change. My height remains, but my hair grows darker, and my skin smoother. Kane appears next to me, his hair short but just as spectacularly messy. We're blurry, at first, but after a moment, the memory becomes clear, playing out into the glass panes in front of me.

"This is a really bad idea," I whispered, anxiously scanning my surroundings. Kane rolls his eyes, the moonlight bathing over his cheekbones.

"It's fine. It's not like I stole the key, Ms. Georgia gave it to me. I can go in and out of the library whenever I want."

My heart pounded heavily in my chest, and I took a steadying breath.

"This is stupid. C'mon, handsome. Can't we just go to Roberta's?" I whined. Kane's hand twisted, the lock of the door clicking open. He paused.

"If you want to go to Roberta's, we can go to Roberta's." He sighed. "But I'm tired of hiding in a dirty, rusty lighthouse all the time. I want to take you to all my favorite places. I want to go on a date. And I know you aren't ready for that, and it's fine. You don't have to be ready. But I stopped going to The Rainbow Club. I don't hold your hand in public. I've given up my pride, because I know you aren't ready, and I love you anyway. This-" He gestured to the library doors in front of us. "This is a compromise. Break the rules, just once, and be with me. Pretend this is a date, and kiss me against the shelves, and I'll play with your hair while you read me Shakespeare, because I can't fucking do it anymore Marcus. I can't just keep fucking you against a lighthouse wall and act like we're barely coworkers in public. I'm losing it. I'm losing myself. And if you don't give me something, anything, you're going to lose me too."

"Are you going in?"

My head whips around to look at a man standing beside me, his fingers gripping the handle.

"Sorry?" I ask, heat rushing to my cheeks as the memory begins to fleet. The man chuckles, gesturing to the door.

"The library. Are you going in? It's starting to rain."

My gaze flashes back to the door, the memory replaced by my own, aged reflection. I don't know that it's someone I like. But it's someone who isn't afraid. Someone who loves without vigilance of the world around him. Someone who writes about it, and celebrates it, and encourages it. Someone who has come so far to accept his type of love, and will be damned if he doesn't do everything he can to save it.

"No." I step back, small droplets of rain beginning to wash over me. "I actually have to go."

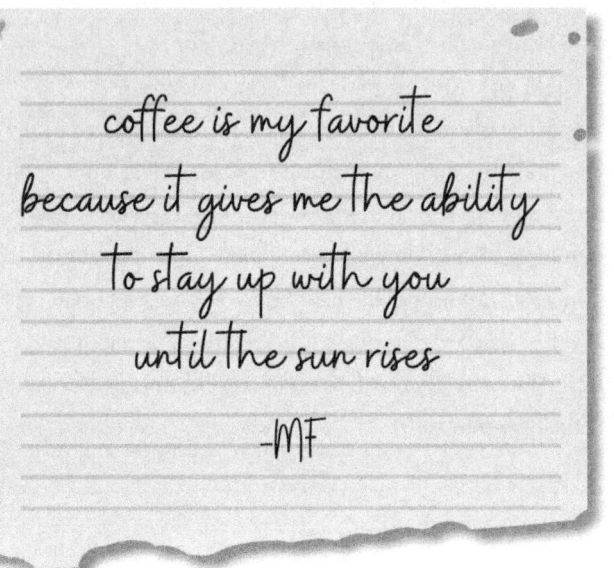

coffee is my favorite
because it gives me the ability
to stay up with you
until the sun rises

-MF

Chapter Thirteen

KANE

My finger traces the spine of the faux, periwinkle book. It's sandwiched between the shelf, and a collector's edition of Sense and Sensibility. I've thought about it many times throughout the years, and walked past it even more, but I haven't touched it until now. Not since stocking the book beside it, and even then, I tried to ensure that the side of my finger never really made contact.

Why I would hold onto something I'm scared to even touch is simple; it contains something valuable. Irreplaceable. Damaging.

So no, I don't touch it. And no, I haven't opened the compartment inside since I closed it twenty years ago. And no, I will never get rid of it.

"He's so *senseless*," Clara huffs from the other side of the bookshelf. She pulls out a stack of books, creating a little window in between the shelves so that she can look at me. "I mean, showing up here is one thing. I bet he really knew you owned the store. But *kissing* you when he's supposed to be apologizing? Leaving a hickey behind like some ridiculous teenager, making his territory?"

I can't be irritated with Clara, because she's only trying to protect me. Her intentions are never anything but pure. Still, I have to take a deep breath before I answer her to make sure my tone isn't snappy.

"To be fair, I kissed him," I remind her. Clara waves her hand in the air dismissively.

"It's not your fault, Kane. He's a dick. I mean, you got your apology, so why else would he bring you to the lighthouse, unless he was planning to screw you?"

Again, Clara's recount of the night is inaccurate. But she did get one thing right. I got my apology from Marcus, so I had no real reason to ask him to walk with me. But I don't know how to explain to her that there was something more I was missing. I *am* missing.

It's outrageous, after everything, that I'd feel so desperate to stay beside him. It's insane that I'd kiss him. And it's completely and utterly ridiculous that I can't stop thinking about him.

Not just the kiss, or his heavy breath. Not only the feel of his hand, or the sense of his presence. But his *voice*. His *words*. I can't stop replaying that sentence, over and over again.

You didn't deserve that.

It isn't profound. It isn't even new. Clara told me that about a hundred times after Marcus left. But for some reason, coming from him, I actually want to believe it.

This entire time, I've been angry with him. But I've also been angry with myself. I hated how much pressure I put on him to go public, to slap a label on it. I hated that I had a family who embraced me, while he was born somewhere love had rules and stipulations. I hated that I couldn't just let it be the way it was. Subtle. Secretive. Casual.

When his parents barged into Well Written Books, screaming at the top of their lungs that I had corrupted their child, that I had forced him into a relationship he could never want, I almost believed them.

I didn't think that I had turned Marcus gay, or forced him to believe he was attracted to men. But I did begin to believe that maybe, I put him in an impossible situation. And I knew for a fact, that it was my fault he was outed. Because had he not been with me, they never would have known.

So when the tears were streaming down my face, and Duke was physically removing them from the property, I couldn't help but think that I deserved it. I deserved to be yelled at, and I deserved to be left. That didn't make me less angry at Marc, though. It just made me more angry at myself.

"He didn't bring me to the lighthouse," I mumble softly, sliding her a book from the stack in my arms. "There was a windstorm."

"Let me be clear, Kane. I'm not mad. I'm just—" She sighs, combing her fingers through her hair. "Confused?"

An airy laugh slips out of me. "Make that two of us."

Clara takes the book I gave her, and props it up on the shelf so that it creates a barrier between us. .

"What are your plans for the evening?" I ask, changing the topic. Clara rounds the corner, now standing beside me as she stares up at the shelves in front of us. The stack of books in her arms have shrunk, and she shifts her weight onto her toes, reaching up to slide a book into an empty spot on the shelf.

"Judah has his sign language class tonight," she reminds me. "But after, Derrick and I were going to take him to the Sand Dollar Creamery. You should come, and bring Dickie too."

I look over at Clara, her silky blonde hair, and soft green eyes. She is such a beautiful person, in every way that matters. And I'm so grateful that if I have to be in this life, I have her by my side.

"I might," I answer. "I'm pretty tired."

Clara glances over at me, her eyes narrowing like she's dissecting my answer. When you're living with depression, "tired" can mean many things. It can mean sleepy, or exhausted, it could mean you're tired of talking, or tired of being in public. Tired of being tired, or tired of life.

In this case, I'm tired of thinking about Marcus. All I want is to go back to last night, and choose to stay instead. To not let "shouldn't" get the best of me. To experience him for the first time in twenty years, and to love every second of it. To tell him that, no matter how pitiful it may be, and no matter how hard I tried to fill it, he's always had a spot in my heart that nobody else could ever occupy.

But you can't rewind time, and after leaving him alone, stranded in the lighthouse, I think Marcus would be perfectly content if he never saw me again.

Clara places a hand gently on my shoulder. "Sand dollar creamery, at seven."

When Clara tasks me with spending time with her, it's like I simultaneously anticipate and dread the event. It doesn't make sense that those two emotions sit in equal parts, but that's something I've learned about depression throughout the years.

It's contradictory.

So I sit in the store, and stare at the clock while the hands inch closer to the number seven. Normally, I'd be reading or cleaning or stocking books. But Clara and I pretty much scrubbed every inch of the place this morning, and during, every book found a home within the shelves. As far as reading goes... I think I need to take a break from false realities, because it's quickly getting me into trouble.

My mind keeps coming up with all these scenarios. Stupid "what-ifs" that could never really happen. Ones where Marcus never left, or where I tracked him down. Some like now, where he comes back and it's like the years apart brought us close together. Those are the best scenarios, because even though they're completely ludicrous, I've convinced myself that they're somehow possible.

Like I said, I need to take a break. Besides, what's next? Vivienne St. James turns out to be my mom?

No thanks. I'd rather sit here, listening to the rain, and mindlessly watching the golden hands tick.

Tick. Tick. Tick.

Tick. Tick. Tick.

Tick. Tick. Ti-

Bang.

An obnoxious rapping erupts from the glass door, startling me, and sending Dickie barreling into the back room, his hind legs dragging behind him. My heart races, pounding incessantly against the inside of my ribcage as I catch my breath, and sink lower into my chair.

It isn't often that customers show up after closing, but when it happens, I typically let them in. Whether I'm feeling nice, or social, or just plain poor, I think it's important to allow access to literature when those who need it are present. Unfortunately for them, while my bank account would appreciate the visit, I most certainly do not.

The blinds are closed. The lights are off. And the neon "open" sign sitting in the window ceases to glow.

Still, the knocking continues, growing even more aggressive.

"Okay! Alright!" I call out, prying myself from my chair. Even with the blinds closed, I can tell how hard the rain is coming down. As my hands grip the doorknob, the sound floods my ears. A million drops pattering against the concrete. The knocking continues, and I pull the door open. "We're closed, actually. But if you really—"

I stop, the words catching in my throat and refusing to move. Marcus stands in front of me, his tall body towering over me, and his grey hair drenched. His breath is rapid, like white water waves, rolling up before their crashing descent. Drops of water drip from his brow bone down the sides of his face, and his large hand reaches out, forcing the door to remain open against the wall.

"I'm sorry," he says breathily. He drags a hand through his hair, the damp strands sticking to his forehead. He looks so hot, and handsome, standing here in the middle of a storm. The way his breath is panting. How his icy eyes are dark, but sincere. How his wet shirt hugs his chiseled chest. I'm envious of the rain, for it pools around his mouth the way I wish I could. "I'm sorry for just showing up like this, I am. But I leave tomorrow and I-" He licks the raindrops off his lips, then continues. "I couldn't leave without seeing you. I had to answer your question."

"My question?" I ask, trying to inhale. I'm breathing, I'm sure of it. But it feels as though there's a hole in my lungs, like a defected balloon. I shake my head.

"In this life," Marcus begins. His chest is still rising and falling, water traveling down every inch of his body, but he doesn't seem to care. My eyes catch onto the green veins in his forearm as he pulls it to his forehead and wipes away the rain. "There is room for you. There's *always* been room for you, Kane. I've made sure of it. You are in every book that I've written. You're in every cup of coffee that I've sipped, and every library that I visit. I see you in every crowd, of every event I've ever been to. Everything that I *am* is because of you. And I know this is crazy, trust me, I'm well aware. But I can't just go back, knowing that I didn't try. Knowing that I didn't tell you the full truth." Droplets settle into the divots of his cheeks, and his chest continues to heave as he stares at me with no intent of ever looking away. "I was standing in front of the library earlier, wondering why the hell the universe would do this. Why it would bring us back together after all these years of being apart. And then it hit me: I never told you the complete and honest truth. *That's* what it is. That's why we're *here*. So that I can tell you what I've always wanted to, with shameless honesty. So here it is: It's you, or nothing Kane. It always has been."

I begin to think the rain is making its way inside the store, until I realize that my cheeks are wet, because I'm crying. Tears pool in my eyes as I listen to Marcus. As I watch his breath move in and out of his body. As the words I've been desperate to hear all these years leave his lips. It's unearthly. Everything I've ever wanted, and yet, I still find myself stepping backwards, my head shaking.

if i pry the batteries
from the clock against the wall
could we just sit here forever
watching time disappear?
-MF

Chapter Fourteen

MARCUS

"No," Kane says, his lip trembling. Rainwater pools onto the hardwood floor of Well Written Books as I step inside, closer to him. He continues shaking his head. "*No*, Marcus. You can't just— You don't get to just show up after all this time and expect me to welcome you with open arms. Not after you left the way you did. You didn't look for me. You didn't even try to reach out. You sat over in the fucking desert on your pillar of success while I was here cleaning up the mess *you* created. I know I kissed you the other night, and I'm sorry if you thought that was anything more than a lapse of judgement. But I can't— *we* can't just pick up like the last twenty years never happened."

Kane's eyes fill with tears as he speaks, and his voice shakes. I take another step closer to him, water pooling up from the soles of my shoes as my weight shifts. But Kane doesn't budge. He doesn't move closer to me, but he doesn't move further away either. And it's that little detail that tells me it isn't time to give up.

Not yet.

"Why not?" I ask it calmly. Coolly. Sincerely. And I think it shocks him that I didn't simply turn away.

That's what I would have done, in the beginning. It's what I always did when he asked for more. But I'm not scared of losing my parents' approval, or being open about my sexuality. The only thing I'm scared of is losing Kane forever.

Kane lets out a humorless laugh, and he looks around the store as if the answers lie within the shelves of it. His tongue clicks against the roof of his mouth until his eyes reluctantly meet mine.

"Because—" An exasperated sigh escapes his lips, and he throws his hands up irately. "They did happen! And now I've changed. And *you've* changed. And things are different, and-"

"And that's exactly what they need to be, Kane. *Different.* Don't you see? We've been given another chance at this. One where I'm out, and you're living. Not just surviving, but *living*, Kane."

"Yeah?" he asks aggressively, his chest heaving. He takes a step closer to me, his pointer finger digging into my sternum. His face is only inches from mine, and I can make out every crease in his skin, and every hair in his beard. "What's the difference between the two, Marcus? Enlighten me, because I have never, not *once*, felt like I've been living."

"You know what your problem is, Kane? Your problem is that you are *addicted* to being sad. You have spent so long feeling the way you feel, that any time another emotion begins to flood your senses, you panic. That's why you read sad books. It's why you watch sad movies. It's why you're *running* from this. Because you know it's what you want, and it scares you that you might actually end up happy. You want to know the difference between living and surviving?"

Kane's breath brushes against my lips, his thick brows furrowed together. "What?"

"The difference is that now, you *want* to want to try. *That's* living. And it isn't always nice, and it's almost never easy. But it's beautiful, and it's messy, and if you allow it to, it will bring you little moments of happiness. They're fleeting, and so easy to miss, but they're *there.* You just have to fucking let them be."

My jaw tenses as my back teeth clench together, my lungs expanding and deflating at a rate so rapid, my vision begins to blur. But my nerves work just the same, and I can feel the pressure of Kane's finger gently lift from my chest.

"You piss me off," he mutters bitterly. His breath paints my lips, and his chest brushes against my ribcage as his lungs expand. I swallow.

"I know."

My hand snakes around the back of his neck, pulling him into me until our lips crash together. Kane, surprisingly, melts into it completely.

"I still hate you," he mumbles through heavy breaths. I fight back a smile as I press my lips against his, my tongue slipping ever so slightly into the cut of his teeth. Feeling him so close to me, tasting his lips in this desirous way, makes all the blood in my face rush to the pulsing cock centered between my thighs.

I suck his bottom lip into my mouth, then let it pop back into place. "Whatever you say, handsome."

Kane's fingers travel to the back of my head, tugging gently on the short strands. As his body presses against mine, his hardened muscle settles between my legs. The pulse of it entices a desperate moan to slip from my lips, and I pull him into me even closer. My back falls against the door, crushing the blinds beneath my weight. Kane's body follows my path, the warmth of his body glued to mine in a breathy heap.

"This is such a bad idea," he whispers airily, running his fingers up the front of my shirt. The soft pads of his fingertips trace the outline of my muscles, drifting over each one like waves crashing over rock.

"Why?" I ask, pushing my hips forward into him. His head tosses back, and he lets out a weak groan.

"Because I'm not going to know how to stop."

I let one arm loose from Kane's waist, drawing it up to his face to brush his soft, brown hair from his wanting eyes. "Then don't."

The blinds beneath me rattle as Kane hastily tugs my shirt over my head. Cool air seeps from the mist-stained door into the skin of my back, but I don't care. I just pull Kane closer to me, allowing his body to warm mine. There is nothing like this polarity, cold and hot, hate and love. It settles a need deep in my stomach, a desire to find the center of it all.

Loud breaths spill from my mouth as Kane attaches his lips to the tender spot on the underside of my jaw. My fingers find the buttons on the front of his shirt, and I quickly, but carefully, undo them, no matter how badly I wish to rip them off instead. As his hair-covered chest exposes, he sucks the sensitive skin into his mouth, forcing a slight wince out of me, and causing the hardened muscle between my legs to jump.

"Sorry," he says, a mischievous smirk tugging at the corners of his mouth. I pull his shirt down his shoulders, and toss it somewhere into the abyss of the shelves.

"Don't lie."

A thick finger dips into the waistband of my pants, tracing along the seam of my briefs. He leans in, his lips grazing against the shell of my ear.

"Okay," he whispers. "I'm not sorry."

Then, his finger travels below the elastic. Slowly. Delicately. Intimately. It paints pictures on my skin, soft circles getting closer and closer to my hardened cock. Tension builds in my jaw as it clenches, my breath hitching while my hips involuntarily buck forward. Kane's beard tickles my cheek, and his hand draws up, hooking his fingers on the band of my briefs, and pulling down gently, the pants above them following. As the fabric falls to my feet, Kane sinks to his knees.

And that's enough.

Just seeing him, kneeling in front of me, staring up with those dark brown, insatiable eyes, is enough to make me collapse. My knees shake as his hand draws up from my ankle to my thigh, tracing delicately along the inside of it before he finally travels over to my throbbing, needy cock. His tawny beige hand wraps around it, and I swear the remainder of the blood in my body all rushes to the muscle gripped within his fingertips. His eyes lock with mine, gazing through that messy brown head of hair as he sticks out his tongue, and gently licks the dripping tip.

"Oh fuck," I whine, one hand steadying my balance against the door as the other feathers his hair between my fingers, gripping it gently. Kane continues, his hand stabilizing the base of my needy cock as his mouth opens wider, taking the first inch of it into his mouth. A wet, warm sensation washes over me, shuddered breaths escaping my trembling lips as he bobs his head, allowing me to go deeper. His tongue is textured, but smooth, and it is the best thing I have ever felt in my entire life. I don't know how I went twenty years without something as delicious and fulfilling as this. But I know I never want to do it again.

"Kane," I mumble. He begins to stroke me gently, taking me out of his mouth and tracing the bulging vein down the side of my length. Then, he glances up at me. "I didn't-" A shaky breath fumbles from my lips, and I remove my hand from his hair, tracing my fingers along his jaw until I reach his chin, tilting it upwards. "I didn't come here to just fuck you. You know that, right? I want— Well I want you forever. I want to do all the things I should have done then. Sit in the window nook and read to you as I stroke your hair. I want to kiss you in the middle of Rita's and tackle you on the beach. I want to write you love letters again. This isn't just... I don't want to do this if it's going to end with me leaving tomorrow and never seeing you again."

Kane stares up at me, a dimpled smile settled into the curve of his lips.

"You're so fucking gay Marcus," he teases, biting the corner of his lip to hide his smile. But it doesn't work, and the most adorable, taunting grin breaks across his face. I roll my eyes, but can feel the tension of my own smile tugging on my lips.

"So gay," I murmur, and Kane's eyes shimmer as he takes me back into his mouth, tipping his head forward until his lips reach the base. I feel the soft ball of flesh in the back of his throat grazing against the tip of my cock as he devours me, fully and entirely. Goosebumps wash over my skin as his throat dances around my dick, soft moans choked back by the thrumming muscle. My desperate groans, however, flow from my mouth loudly each time Kane comes back for more. It's cosmic, the way my tip grows raw and sensitive, tingling against his warm tongue. What an exceptional idiot I was to ever give this up.

Tension builds in my core as Kane's throat vibrates against me. My cock constricts at the sensation, every muscle in my body tightening as well. My heart pounds so loud I can't hear the rain against the door or the rattle of the blinds behind me. The only sound funneling into my ears is the repetitive *thump, thump, thump.* It gets faster as my breath increases, rapid air moving in and out of my lungs as if it were never really there at all. My eyes squeeze shut as Kane thrusts my cock into the very back of his throat, causing everything around me to go dark. Stars fill the galaxy forming behind my eyelids, white shining spots spreading and moving as Kane's hand follows the path of his lips. My core grows tighter, and I tug desperately at the hair now gripped between my fingers as I feel myself tip. Like I've been standing at the edge of a cliff, toes hovering over the jagged ridge, until finally, I just fall. My toes curl, digging into the hardwood floor as needy prayers tumble from my lips.

"Fuck Kane," I moan, still staring at the kinetic stars around me. "I need you. Holy fuck, I need you so badly." Kane's pace quickens, and one hand travels to the underside of my cock, gently squeezing my balls between his warm, sweating palms. "Oh god, just like that, Kane. Don't stop."

Kane obeys, massaging the soft, tender balls of flesh while his mouth continues the synchronous dance of his tongue against my muscle. And just as his thumb grazes my perinium, I feel it. The rock beneath my feet crumbles, and something inside of my stomach pulls so tight, it feels as though it may explode. And then, as the stars around me turn into white, blinding light, Kane pulls back, settling my tip onto his tongue, and stroking me as he swallows the cum that streams from my release. My eyes open, my knees buckling as I absorb the affair, watching as he devours every drop of the hot substance. It pools around the left corner of his lip, and Kane stares up at me hungrily as I take my trembling hand, swipe the droplet with my thumb, then suck it gently into my mouth.

"I need you," he says, in a breathy, needy moan. "Now, please."

devour me completely
every bead of my sweat
every drop of my soul
until, together, we become one

-MF

Chapter Fifteen

KANE

I haven't felt this desperate in forever. It's insatiable, and taunting. Humiliating. There is nothing I should want less than to feel Marcus fully. To give him the chance to reverse all those years of silence and space. But I can't stop playing his words in my mind as he pins me against the shelves, tugging aggressively on the belt loops of my pants.

I want you forever.

And fuck, I hate that I do too. It would be so much easier if I hated Marcus the way I pretend to. If I resented him more than I resent myself. It would make things simple if I could just say, with complete and utter honesty, that I prefer life without him in it. But the words could leave my lips a million times, and they would never get closer to being the truth.

The truth is that for every hour of resentment that exists between Marcus and I, another day was spent in complete and total love with him. I realize it, now, with his lips pressed to my neck, my hands clutching the wooden shelves behind us, that there was never a single second of my life where I didn't love Marcus Fraund, entirely, embarrassingly, and infinitely.

"Are you sure you want this, handsome?" he asks. His breath tickles the crook of my neck, and something about him asking me, with complete care and earnestness, makes me only want it more. A short, humorous breath seeps from my lungs as my hips tilt forward, pressing myself into Marcus' exposed body. My fingers glide over his chiseled abdomen, tracing the valleys etched between each prominent muscle. He's built like a marble statue, flawlessly carved. His hardened cock presses into my soft stomach as I grind against him, causing the muscle to jump needily.

"I need you," I whisper, and Marcus takes the answer for exactly what it is. A plea for pleasure, a primal wanting. His lips crush into mine, his arms wrapping around me as he stumbles backwards. I love the way his bare chest feels pressed against mine. The skin is smooth, and bare, completely opposite from the black hairs strewn across mine. In fact, almost everything about Marcus is opposite of me. He towers about six inches above my head, and where his stomach is carved and muscular, mine bulges out slightly, soft and pliable. I think that's what I find so attractive about him. We are made from different compounds, and different experiences. He is nothing like me, and yet, he can so clearly see the thoughts buried in my mind. Better yet, he can comprehend them.

Paper and pencils crash onto the ground as Marcus swipes his arm across the desk to clear it. My heart rattles against my ribcage as I feel my ass push against the top of the desk, and Marcus presses a hand to my bare chest, pushing me gently so that my weight falls back, and I sit on it. His fingers fumble with the button on the front of my pants, hastily tugging them off while his lips trail behind them. When his teeth sink into my thigh, my pulsing cock twitches, and my head tosses back in a desperate moan.

"I've missed this for so long," I manage to say, though my words are airy and breathless. It's a mortifying thing to admit, that all these years I've been craving him specifically. But if flushed cheeks and slight humbleness is the sacrifice for Marcus fucking me, I will go through red-faced humiliation every day of my life.

His lips travel up my body, from my legs, to the crook of my thigh, up my stomach, and settling against my ear. "Sorry I'm late."

Cold metal from the knob of the drawer sinks into the back of my bare leg as Marcus' hands journey down my exposed body. I begin to shift underneath him, ready to endure whatever embarrassment necessary to feel him inside of me. His full, hardened length pounding me until I melt into a useless, begging puddle. But just as my body begins to turn, realization washes over me.

"I don't—" I swallow nervously, dryness tugging at the base of my throat. "I don't have a condom."

Marcus stops, his wandering hands hovering over my curved waist. I hold my breath, ready to kick myself for being so.... so... *celibate*. It didn't occur to me to make a stop at the corner grocery, because I didn't think Marcus and I would end up here. I didn't think I'd end up here with *anyone*, in fact, as the last time I had sex was years ago. But something shimmers in Marcus' eyes, and he locates his pants, digging in the pocket until he finally pulls out a worn, leather wallet.

"I've got one," he says, taking a little silver packet from the folds. A smile breaks across his face, and I force a return, even though something in my gut sinks.

It's not like I expected Marcus to be as *inactive* as I've been. He's always needed that physical touch, the fulfillment of his desires. But the thought tugs at the corners of my mind like a torture device. It shouldn't, because if all Marcus wanted to do was fuck me, well, he'd have had his way the first day he walked back into my life. Still, it settles in, seeping into every ridge and every crease like a plague.

"Are you okay?" he asks, his smile fading. I look up at him, sucking in a nervous breath and nodding my head.

"Yeah, no. I'm good," I reply. But Marcus' frown deepens.

"Do you still want to? We don't have to—"

"I want to."

He approaches me, his bare body glistening in the warm lights. "What is it, Kane?"

I shake my head, but my eyes fixate on the foil square between his fingers. "Nothing."

Marcus stands in front of me, his body wedged carefully between my thighs as he stabilizes himself with one hand on the desk, and uses the other to gently trace my jaw.

"Kane," he says softly.

"Hmm?"

Goosebumps spread from the corner of my jaw, where his skin touches mine, all the way across my body. I can feel them on the back of my neck, and down my arms. Across my chest and below my stomach.

"We haven't touched in twenty years, and I was still in love with you for every minute of it. I could never touch you again, and not a single thing about my feelings for you would change."

The knot building in my stomach, the puppet strings tugging on my brain, all of it suddenly snaps when Marcus speaks those words, the doubt that filled my body dissipating. I look into his eyes, greeted with nothing but pure sincerity and care, and even if this were my last day on Earth, it would also be my favorite. His thumb glides gently over my bottom lip, and heat funnels to my growing erection.

"Touch me," I say, maintaining eye contact. Marcus' jaw tenses, and he tries to hide it, but a subtle smile forms in the groove of his lips.

"Yeah?" he whispers, but strongly, with confidence. His brow quirks as he leans into me, his thumb still tracing along my bottom lip. "Do you want me, handsome?"

After this, after *everything*, Marcus calling me "handsome" shouldn't affect me how it does. That stupid, burning sensation filling my cheeks, the soft flutter in my stomach, it's all so ridiculous. And addictive. And I will do anything to hear him say it again.

I nod needily, my throat bobbing as I swallow. "I want you so bad, Marc. Please, fuck me."

Marcus' chin tilts up, that stupid smirk sewn into his sculpted cheeks. He leans in even closer, his lips grazing my ear as he whispers lowly:

"Such a needy one, aren't you, handsome?"

Oh fuck.

I tug my hips to the side, hoping Marcus takes the hint that a dull ache has begun to form inside of me. He listens, tearing open the foil wrapper, and sliding on the lubricated condom. After, he grabs my hips and turns my body so that my abdomen is pressed against the edge of the desk. His hand snakes up my back, tracing the hair at the base of my neck before gently nudging me downwards. I comply, bending my body so that my ass is pressed against Marcus' large, thick cock, and all my weight shifts to my torso, leaning over the desk.

"Such a pretty little ass," he murmurs, spitting in his hand before swiping his wet fingers against the rim. My hips tilt back toward him, silently pleading for him to fuck me. But Marcus takes it slow, grinding is dick gently against the hole while he trails soft kisses down my back. I forgot what it's like, to make love. There is nothing like it, being so open and vulnerable to someone, offering them everything and they choose to do it all with attentiveness. I feel the blood rushing to his length as he grinds it against me.

"God, Marcus." My head tosses back as I put pressure against him, feeling the ridge of his tip glide against my aching rim in a steady rhythm. "Please."

Marcus spits in his hand again, rubbing it gently around the area before he wraps his palm around my hip, centers himself, and slowly pushes into me. A wave of sensation immediately washes over me as Marcus' thick cock stretches me open. I gasp as he gently, but firmly, presses himself deeper until his tip grazes against the sensitive spot inside me, a load moan bubbling from my lips.

"That's it, handsome." He says, his voice prideful but sly. Eagerly, I shift myself backwards to beg for more, and Marcus doesn't hesitate to give it to me. He slides in deeper, causing me to groan and grip the sides of the desk to stabilize myself. "You sound so pretty when you're taking me."

Then, his pace picks up. Feeling Marcus grind against me earlier was like waves crashing onto the shore. But feeling him like this, deep and fast and desperate? It's a heavenly tsunami, and I hope I fucking drown. My muscles clench as Marcus grips my hips, thrusting into me harder and faster than before. A loud, ravenous groan escapes him as his thick shaft pushes deeper, like he's trying to fit every inch of him inside of me.

"You take it so well," he grunts, his thick biceps flexing. A pressure begins to build in my ass, and I cry out as Marcus pulls back, then thrusts himself into me, deep and rough. One palm leaves my hips while the other hangs on, his nails curling into the skin as it pulls me in tighter. With his free hand, he runs his fingers through my hair, tugging so that my head slightly pulls back. "God, that's it, handsome. Are you almost there?"

I nod desperately, my stomach flipping as the feathery ache in my cock intensifies. I tighten around him again, feeling his full girth and length inside of me as the pressure begins to tighten. Like a thread tied into a million knots, forming into one, entangled mass.

"I need to hear you say it, Kane."

"I'm close!" I cry, my knuckles turning white as they continue gripping the desk's edge. "Fuck Marcus, I'm- I'm—" Words don't seem to work when Marcus is fucking me the way that he does. My eyes roll back, and the desk rattles beneath us as he pounds into me with such force, I swear I can't breathe. More tangles form in that giant knot in my stomach, and one hand releases the edge of the desk, traveling down to stroke my aching, pulsing length.

"Fuck, I love you," Marcus moans loudly, tugging harder at my hair on the back of my head. I feel his cock constricting inside of me, my own throbbing in my palm as I stroke it intensely. Heat fills my ass and something tugs, and pulls, and yanks on that ball of thread forming inside of me until finally, it snaps.

Loud, breathy moans spill from both Marcus and I, his grip on my hip stiffening as he pumps into me one last time. My entire body convulses, securing around his cock as streams of cum shoot out of me, my eyes clenching shut as I collapse onto the white, wet mess on the desk in front of me. Euphoria floods me entirely as I lay there in a sweaty, panting heap. Feeling Marcus fuck me, hard, but lovingly, was something I didn't realize I missed so terribly. Marcus exhales slowly, before pulling out of me, and placing a warm kiss against the back of my skull.

"You're incredible," he murmurs, letting his warm body rest innocently against mine. I smile, feeling his weight above me like a therapeutic blanket of foreign familiarity. I breathe out slowly, my eyes trailing up the wall, to the clock who just witnessed the fucking of the century.

"Oh fuck!" I jump back, but I am no match for the weight of Marcus' body. He quickly pulls off of me, a worried expression sewn into his face. Those grey brows pinch together, and he pulls me to my feet with a concerned gaze.

"What? What's wrong?"

I shake my head, tugging open the desk drawer to pull out a roll of paper towels. "I'm supposed to meet Clara, Derrick, and Judah in ten minutes," I explain, using the dry towels to wipe the sticky residue off my body. Marcus' concern quickly turns into humor, and he chuckles richly, ripping a towel off the roll and helping me clean myself up. I scowl, even though I like how the dry, roughness of the paper feels against my skin when Marcus is the one behind it.

"Oh, come on. It's funny," he insists, tossing the used napkin into the garbage. I shake my head.

"It's *not*. There's towels in the back room. Can you please get one wet and bring it to me?"

After my body is cleaned, and the desk is thoroughly sanitized, Marcus and I get dressed as quickly as we got undressed. I toss him his shirt from across the room, and he pulls my briefs from my pants, draping them over the chair.

"I really have to go," I say, shoving my feet into my shoes. I push all my weight into them so that the corner which has bent inward, finally pops back up. "I'm sorry."

Marcus shakes his head, a sickly sweet smile taking over his face as he walks closer to the door. "Don't be. Look, we have to figure this whole thing out. So, can I meet you here tomorrow before I leave? Would that be alright with you?"

My stomach should sink at the offer. Last time Marcus was supposed to meet me at the store, well, I never saw him again. But I know this is different. So instead, heat swells in my chest as I look into his eyes, and I bite my lip gently, nodding.

"Yes, Marcus. That would be fine."

Fine? Really? No, Kane, you idiot. It would be amazing. It would be perfect. It would be everything on the better side of 'fine'.

Marcus smiles, reaching for the handle, and pushing the door open. The rain has stopped, no sounds of pattering droplets to flood the silence between us. And I think, because of that, it burns brighter. I watch him take a step through the frame, and the moment his second foot moves, I find that my feet are moving too.

"Wait!" I call out, catching the door before it slams. Marcus spins around, his luminescent eyes round and confused, like a little lost puppy. I've spent enough of this reencounter with him hesitating, so I don't do it anymore. I stand on my toes, cup his cheeks, and press my lips against his.

The kiss is soft, and warm, and everything about it says "I'll see you tomorrow."

When we finally break away, Marcus looks down at me with blissful confusion. A loud, thrumming noise washes over me as my heartbeat intensifies with the knowledge of what I'm about to say.

"I love you too."

"Nope!" I exclaim, dropping to my knees the second I catch sight of the deceased crustacean flattened atop the road. Completely disregarding my command, Dickie sucks the dead animal into his smushed mouth, and I groan in disgust. "Dickie! Spit it out!" My finger sweeps the back of his throat, prying the crab from his tight jaws. "That thing is in rigor mortis! Your food is fresher than that!"

The roadkill pops free from his jaw, landing onto the sidewalk. I feel guilty, but I kick it to the side as I search the creamery patio for my family.

"Kane!" Clara calls out, tipping her three-scoop-tall ice cream cone in my direction. I look down at the flattened crab one last time, my stomach dipping as I walk away from it.

"Hey! You made it." Derrick dances as he sings the words, lifting a spoon of ice cream to Judah's lips. But the second Judah's eyes lock onto Dickie and I, he swings his arms open, sending the ice cream, and spoon in which it sat upon, flying across the patio. A chuckle escapes me, and I allow Dickie to lick up the creamy puddle as I toss the plastic spoon and grab a new one.

"I'm happy to see you too," I sign to Judah, as I sit in an empty seat at the table. "But I don't go throwing stuff about it."

Judah giggles, a toothless grin breaking across his face.

"He's gonna be a javelin thrower, I think," Derrick declares, taking the yellow plastic spoon from my hand and nodding in appreciation. "Can I get you something? They have this strawberry sorbet. It's really good."

"I'm allergic to strawberry, actually," I explain. "But thank you." I turn to Clara, analyzing the tower of flavors piled onto her cone. "What did you get?"

Her tongue drags across the top layer, light green ice cream gathering onto the tip of it. "Pistachio, cherry, and—" Clara looks over at me, her eyes instantly narrowing as she fully absorbs the sight in front of her. "Kane?"

"Yes?"

"Why do you have sex hair?"

My brows furrow, my stomach sinking. "What?" I laugh nervously, running a hand through my sweaty, messy locks. "I don't have sex hair."

My gaze drifts to Derrick, who just finished shoveling a giant scoop of sorbet into his mouth.

"Don't look at me," he says, his mouth still full. "She was with you for seventeen years. If my wife says you have sex hair-" He eyes me up and down. "Then you *have* sex hair."

Heat floods my cheeks as I continue messing with the strands on my head, tossing and tugging them until I feel like they're "normal messy" and not "sex messy."

"Nope!" Clara huffs, biting the remainder of the top scoop into her mouth. Her voice is muffled by the ice cream, but I can still make out her disapproving tone. "Too late."

"I *don't* have sex hair!" I say defensively. Clara's eyes lock onto Derrick's, then they both stare at me skeptically.

"I'm not judging." Derrick shrugs. "I saw that one coming from a mile away."

"What one?" Clara asks, her head whipping around. She stares at him for a moment, until her eyes widen and her jaw drops. She shakes her head vigorously.

"*No*," she pleads. "Tell me you didn't!"

I swallow anxiously, my throat growing suddenly dry. There's no use in lying to Clara. If this whole thing works out, she'll have to accept it at some point. And if it doesn't? Well, she'll need to know so that she can help put me back together again.

I sigh. "It's complicated."

Clara laughs manically. "You're telling me. You know what's *'com-plicated'* Kane? Spending twenty years doing everything you can to help your best friend heal, just to watch him undo all of it for some nostalgic hookup! *That's* complicated, and I don't want to go through the process from the beginning. I will, *we* will—" She gestures between her and Derrick. "—because we love you. But I can't just sit back and watch you make a bad choice on a whim."

Weight fills my stomach until it finally begins its descent to the floor. A tightening sensation starts in the side of my chest, then branches out like a tree moving in every possible direction. Clara has done so much for me throughout our lives. If I'm being completely honest, I don't think I would still be alive if it weren't for her. I don't want to be any more of a burden than I already am. I just want her to be happy.

But I want to be happy too. And with Marcus, it feels like I might have an actual shot.

"So is it?" Derrick asks, bouncing Judah carefully on his knee. I glance up at him, noticing the smallest upturn of his lips. I tilt my head, confused.

"Is what?"

"Is it a whim?" he clarifies. His hand travels over to Clara's, squeezing it gently. A soft smile slowly appears on her face, and she looks over to me expectantly.

I let out a controlled breath. "I don't think it's a whim," I answer truthfully, and both Clara and Derrick's smiles silently deepen. "It's a realization." Seconds after the words leave my mouth, Clara stands up, releasing Derrick's hand but still gripping her half-consumed ice cream cone. I frown. "Where are you going?"

Her left brow raises slightly, like the answer is so obvious.

"I'm getting you some ice cream, Kane. Because you're about to tell us *everything*."

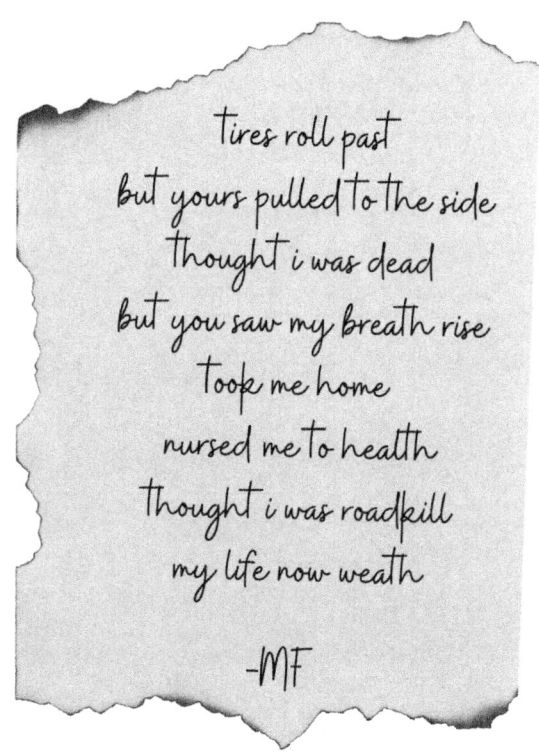

tires roll past
but yours pulled to the side
thought i was dead
but you saw my breath rise
took me home
nursed me to health
thought i was roadkill
my life now weath

-MF

Chapter Sixteen

MARCUS

J anelle grabs an armful of dirty clothes off the bathroom floor, balls it up, and begins shoving it into my suitcase.

"If we leave in ten minutes," she says breathily, squishing the clothing flat. "We will still have enough time to stop by Well Written on the way to the airport."

I pull a worn, bleach-stained sweatshirt over my head, tugging it down over my exposed torso. I don't have the time to look put together today.

"We have to have time," I say seriously. "I can't not go."

Janelle digs through my toiletry bag, tossing me a comb before zipping it up and tucking it into my suitcase.

"We'd have *plenty* of time if you set your alarm." She says it teasingly, but it is no teasing matter. I have to see Kane before I leave. I *have* to.

"I set one, it just didn't go off," I grunt, plopping a pair of sandals into the suitcase. I grab the first pair of pants I see, and drop my pajamas to the floor, stepping out of them. My chest begins to tighten as my breath picks up, each one shorter than the last. "Jesus, what is wrong with me?"

Nellie stops, allowing me to pull my pants up before placing a hand on my shoulder.

"It's going to be okay," she insists. A notification rings from her phone, and she pulls it out of her pocket, checking it. "Look, our driver is here early. Fix your hair, and I'll take your shit downstairs. Okay?" Her warm, dark eyes look up at me and I can't help but find a sense of calm within them. Nellie has always had that effect on me, no matter how often she pisses me off. I nod.

"Yeah, okay. Thank you, Nellie."

She smiles, putting her weight onto the suitcase as she tugs the zipper closed. "Yeah, yeah. Just give me a good Christmas bonus, huh?"

"Oh, was the Mercedes last year not enough for you?" I roll my eyes, combing my hair quickly in the mirror.

"I was thinking more like a Porsche this year," she jokes. "Or a Lambo. Your choice!"

She slams the door shut, and I finish gathering the rest of my things before racing downstairs to meet her. The trunk to the Uber slams closed just as I step outside, and I waste no time tossing myself into the back seat next to Nellie.

"Mr. Lovett." EJ's voice is like nails on a chalkboard as it fills my ears, and I quickly turn to look into the rearview mirror, my eyes catching his. I swallow.

"EJ."

Janelle looks between us, until her gaze narrows onto EJ's reflection, and realization washes over her. She quickly cuts in.

"Look, EJ. We're in a real hurry. So if you could get us to Well Written Books as quickly as possible, it would be much appreciated."

She tacks on her infamous fake smile, those pearly whites a devil in disguise.

"As soon as you buckle up, miss, I'll take you there," EJ shoots back. Janelle glances at her seatbelt, blood rushing to her cheeks as she silently pulls it over her body. When that confirming click echoes through the car, EJ veers out of the parking lot onto the road. As he drives, I stare out my window, silently scripting what I'm going to say to Kane.

How I'm going to move back, and stay with him forever. How I will spend the rest of my life making up for all those years we've missed. How I love him like the stars love the night, like waves love the shore, like words love the page. How he makes me feel unforgettable.

Houses pass me in slow-motion, the sea-salt air misty and thick. But as we round a familiar curve, my eye catches onto something set back from the road. A house. A balcony. A person standing upon it.

It's a bit far, and somewhat hidden by the fog, but I recognize it entirely, and the person outside of it? I think I might recognize her too. Something constricts deep in my chest, and it feels like all the wind has been knocked out of me. I don't have time to think about what I am doing. I just grab the handle of the door, and take a deep breath.

"Stop the car!" I command, much louder than necessary. EJ doesn't hesitate, the brakes squealing as he veers off to the side of the road.

"Jesus, Lovett! Are you serious!" he shouts. "We could have crashed."

I don't even think about processing the words leaving his mouth. I just tug the handle, pushing the door open to be greeted with humid air. A set of thin fingers wrap around my bicep, Janelle's long, pink nails decorating my stained grey sleeves.

"Marcus, we *have* to go. We don't have time to—"

"I'm sorry." I tug away from her, jumping out of the car. "I'll be fast, I promise. I have to— I'll be fast."

Janelle nods, and her face disappears as I slam the door closed behind me. Barreling up the steps to the house, my heart races as my mind spins. I didn't think I'd ever want the opportunity to confront my parents, much less have the opportunity. But seeing my mother up there on the balcony, it's unmistakable. They've been here, in the same goddamned house, this entire time, and never even considered trying to find me. Trying to bring me home. To mend fences. To accept me, and love me, like parents are supposed to do.

I don't want revenge. And at this point, I don't even want their support. I just want them to know, that despite their best efforts, I am still queer. And they will have to live, for the rest of their lives, with the fact that they raised a gay son who is happier than they could have ever dreamed of being.

The sound of my pulse fills my eardrums as I pound on the door, my hands shaking and my shoulders vibrating. I take a deep breath, slow and controlled, but just as the air begins to funnel the bottom of my lungs, that giant red door swings open, a woman standing in its place.

"Hi! Can I help you?" she asks. It definitely isn't my mother. She is much too young. But something about her is familiar, and as I stare at her, I quickly realize why.

"You're the waitress," I say, breathy and confused. The woman nods, an awkward smile creeping across her face.

"Umh.. yeah?"

I shake my head. "Sorry, it's just— Is Deborah Fraund here, by chance? She used to live here and I thought I saw—" The woman's brows weave together, and her face slowly drops. I let out a shaky breath. "Could you at least give her a message for me?"

"I'm sorry, but—" The woman shakes her head. "Deborah died two years ago. Her husband David is here, but he's asleep. I could go get him if—"

"No, no, don't wake him. Just, give him a message for me will you? Are you his caretaker, or?" My hands gesture in no specific manner, beads of water from the air pooling at my hairline. I feel one begin to drip down the side of my cheek, and I brush it off onto my shoulder.

The woman, however confused she may be, smiles sweetly. "Sure, I can take a message," she says, her voice soft and silky. She sticks her hand out to greet me. "I'm Brandy, his daughter."

My hand reaches out to grab hers, until the words fully process in my brain. And the moment they do, my lungs deflate completely, and my stomach bottoms out. I step back, rubbing the back of my head as I stare at the woman in front of me.

It doesn't make sense. I'm an only child. I've always been an only child.

Always.

I clear my throat, the air around my growing colder as all the blood rushes from my cheeks. "Daughter?" I manage to croak. Brandy nods, flashing me a beaming grin.

"The one and only!"

My gaze drifts to her features, and sudden realization begins to flood my body, every hair on my skin standing tall as goosebumps wash over me.

It's true. The divot in the center of her chin, the tall, slender build. It all makes sense now, why she felt so familiar at Rita's. Brandy is the spitting image of my mother. How the fuck did I not see it before?

I step back, my foot slipping down onto the concrete steps as I continue taking in short breaths. This is fucked. This is all *so* fucked.

"Do you mind if—" I shake my head, knowing I shouldn't ask, but I do it anyway. "Do you mind if I ask how old you are?"

Brandy's brows, once again furrow, but an intrigued smile stretches across her face.

"Nineteen."

All the oxygen is pulled from my lungs the second the word leaves her lips. I tumble back, nearly falling as I slip onto the sidewalk behind me. I can feel my pulse in every one of my senses, and my mouth begins to tingle with a metallic taste. Brandy's smile falters.

"Sir? The message?"

I couldn't respond to her even if I tried. I know for a fact, the only thing that will leave my mouth right now if I open it, are eardrum-shattering sobs. So I don't. I don't respond, and I don't open my mouth. I breathe through my nose as I sprint back to the car, tears streaming down the center of my cheeks.

"Jesus Christ, Marcus! What the hell happened?" Janelle immediately wraps her arm around me, using the other hand to pull my seatbelt over my shaking body. She pats the back of EJ's seat, signaling for him to drive away, before turning back to me, squeezing me tightly. "Marcus, are you okay?"

Completely humiliated, I pat my face dry, forcing myself to stare at the roof of the car and taking controlled breaths until the tears finally cease. I don't answer her until I know that when I do, my voice won't come off fragile and weak. Swelling forms around my eyes, my cheeks following in a splotchy, puffy display. One last, shaky breath slips from my lips, just as the car makes a turn that I know to be wrong.

"We're supposed to be going to Well Written," I say, my tone still not as confident as I would have liked it to sound. Nellie looks at me sympathetically, her hand gently brushing my shoulder.

"We're going to miss our flight," she replies softly. I shake my head, my brows furrowed as my breathing begins to quicken again.

"No. No, we have to go to Well Written. I have to see Kane. I have to—"

"Marcus." Janelle's voice is so much more controlled than mine. Her tone is steady, and caring, but also firm. I fucking hate it when it's firm. "We can't miss this flight. We have a *very* important signing that we can't miss. And—"

"Fuck the signing!" I throw my hands up into the air, my vision growing blurry as tears begin to well again. "Fuck the signing, fuck the publishers, and fuck Simeon! Okay? Just fuck it!"

"It doesn't just affect *you*, Marcus," Janelle snaps. Her nostrils flare, but she pauses for a moment before continuing, like she's still carefully considering her next words. "I'm sorry, but it doesn't. It affects me too, and I would really like to not piss off the people who are going to cut my checks someday. And I know you're in that position now, and I'm grateful for everything you do. I am. But I put up with a lot of bullshit to get here. So please—" Her eyes catch mine, and the anger drains from her face, replaced with sincere worry. "Please, can we just call him? Write him an email? Explain what happened? You can fly right back here after the meeting, just— write him an email. Okay?"

I stare into those deep brown eyes, round and tired. Janelle is right. I put her through a lot. Every single day, there is something I do that makes her life more difficult. And sure, I pay her. And of course, I reward her with outrageously expensive gifts and free trips around the globe. But Janelle would trade all of that for a good reputation in the publishing industry. And if we miss, or push, or skip one more meeting or event, that reputation is going to follow her for the rest of her career.

I nod silently, swiping at the tears trailing down my cheeks.

"I don't know his number," I sniffle. "What's the email?"

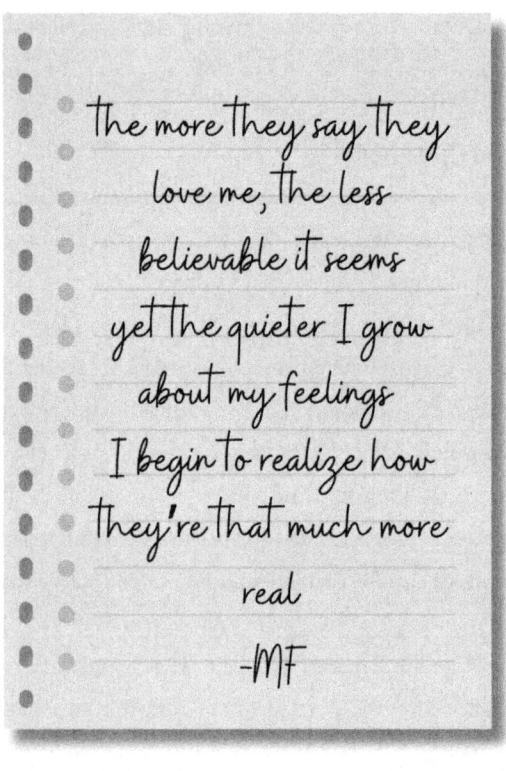

the more they say they
love me, the less
believable it seems
yet the quieter I grow
about my feelings
I begin to realize how
they're that much more
real

-MF

Chapter Seventeen

KANE

9:27AM

The scent of espresso fills my nose as Clara hands me the warm cup of coffee, steam rolling off the top in light, rippled waves. The heat from the cup burns into my palm, but I don't notice. I just continue staring at the clock. Every time that the hands tick, my stomach tightens, and an acidic flavor anxiously rises from the back of my throat.

"Are you *sure* he's coming?" Clara asks, lifting a screwdriver to the corners of the shelves. I look over at her, pushing my reading glasses up the bridge of my nose. It's not as if the thought hasn't crossed my mind. Of course, with Marcus' past, leaving abruptly with no contact, well, it would be stupid of me to not at least consider the idea. But everything about these last three days, hell, about these last ten years, gives me reasonable hope. Marcus is just the right amount of different.

His confidence has carried to his identity, and it shows. In his work, his voice, even his mannerisms. He used to walk around with the constant sense that he was being observed, perceived as someone he knew his parents wouldn't approve of. I remember how he'd constantly adjust his posture, and alter his dialogue to match the younger men around us. But there was none of that the past three days. He was wholly and completely himself, the way I always wished he'd be.

"He's coming," I answer. "He said he would."

Clara's hand falls to her side, and she approaches me with a sincere smile. "If you say he's coming, then I believe you. I just don't want to see you get hurt again."

I nod appreciatively, fighting the urge to glance at the clock for the hundred-thousandth time today. "I need a distraction."

Her brow cocks, her head tilting. "What kind of distraction?"

"I don't know," I shrug. "I just can't keep sitting here, staring at the clock while I wait for him to stop by. Have we put in August's order yet?"

"Nope. I still can't log into the email."

I frown. "Can't we just reset the password or something?"

"We could." She nods. "If Derrick didn't accidentally put my contact information on one of those spam websites forcing me to get a new number."

I groan, tossing my weight back in the chair and letting it roll a few inches away from the desk. God, this desk. I don't think I'll ever be able to look at it the same way after what went down last night. I don't know if I should burn it, or cherish it forever.

"Alright, well, we've got to call them and figure that out soon," I say. Clara shoots me an unimpressed glance, her brows raised in a way that tells me she's calling bullshit.

"You mean *I* need to call them," she replies cunningly. A guilty grin creeps across my face.

"Exactly."

Her eyes roll but a reluctant smile tugs at the corners of her lips. She sighs. "Whatever would you do without me?"

"Die, probably."

A fluttery laugh slips from her lips, and she smacks me lightly, then gestures for me to follow her. "Shut up. Come help me with this."

11:53AM

"Wait, so how did Marcus find out where you live?" Clara asks, fluffing Dickie's bed and setting it on the window nook. He looks up at her with a noticing gaze, pacing back and forth as he waits to be lifted. He can jump up there just fine, he just prefers the chariot ride. I suck in a nervous breath, my gaze darting back to the desk. My cheeks flush, but I pretend to notice something invisible in the corner that needs my attention. "Kane?"

I try to fight it, but my eyes greet Clara's with a guilty shine. The smile planted on her face fades, a slightly disgusted, but more so disappointed expression consuming it.

"Wait, that all happened *here*?!" She exclaims, her nose wrinkling. "Gross." She lifts Dickie onto his pedestal. He plops down onto his bed, stretching out to bask in the sunlight as he lets out a content groan.

"Homophobe," I tease, and Clara props her hands on her hips disapprovingly.

"Oh don't even start with me." She blows a tendril of blonde hair from her face. "Fucking in the bookstore is gross no matter what gender the fuckers are. *Fuckees?* You know what I mean." Her hands fall to the nook bench, moving it back and forth causing it to rattle and creak. "This thing needs to be replaced."

I nod, running a hand through my hair. "Want to do it after closing?" I ask. She kicks it lightly, and I swear it sounds like something inside it snaps.

"Sure. I can swing by the hardware store later. The frame feels fine, I think it's just the plywood that needs to be replaced." Her fingertips trace the splintered edge, then draw up to scratch Dickie on the butt.

Silence settles between us. It's something I've been trying to avoid all morning, because even though we hashed it out last night, I still feel like Clara thinks I'm insane. And maybe I am. But I'd rather be crazy with Marcus, than perfectly sane without him. I just need to find the right words to explain that to her.

"I know you think it's ridiculous," I say finally, breaking the silence. Her brows immediately pinch together, and she shakes her head.

"No, I don't." I shoot her an unconvinced look, and the valley between her brows disappears. "Okay, a *little* bit. But you have to admit, Kane. This is all so..." She trails off, and I lean my weight against a wooden shelf, crossing my arms.

"Sudden?"

Her lip curls and her head bops around like she's trying to make an important decision. "Well... *yeah.*"

I nod, letting a slow breath blow from my lips. "I know it is, Claire. I'm not going to sit here and deny that this isn't batshit crazy, because it is. But—" I swallow, chewing on the inside of my cheek. Clara's shoulders sink down, and she walks over to me, wiping a set of crumbs from the collar of my shirt.

"But you love him," she cuts in, her jade green eyes locking with mine. I nod slowly, letting the word seep into my skin like oil. It's true. I know it is, otherwise, I wouldn't have said it last night. But hearing it come from someone who knows me, someone who cares so much she'd take any chance to deny it? Well, it feels even more vivid. Undeniably real.

"Yeah," I admit. "I love him. And Clara?"

"Hmm?"

I nervously pick at the skin around my thumb nail. "I really think he loves me too."

Her hand settles onto my shoulder, the coolness of her palm traveling through the fabric to my skin, and she smiles.

"You know, Kane," she says quietly, her eyes shining. "I think so too."

"Yeah?" I ask, a hint of confusion in my tone. Clara hates Marcus for what he did, and that opinion hasn't seemed to magically change in the last three days. But she smiles, and pats my shoulder gently.

"I think he always has. I just didn't think he'd ever stop running from it."

3:05 PM

I can't deny that I'm starting to grow anxious about Marcus' arrival. I should have asked when I could've expected him last night, but I was in such a hurry the thought didn't even cross my mind. Now, I wish it had, because it would have saved me some truly unnecessary stress.

Marcus is going to come. I know he is. There would be no other reason for him to do all of this. To invite me to dinner, to profess his love, to arrange this meeting before he leaves. Not unless he's one, sadistic fuck. And I'd like to think I know him well enough to vouch that he's not.

Still, that doesn't stop the hole burning through my chest right now. It doesn't prevent the knot, twisting and tugging in my stomach every time a customer walks through the door, and I lift my head to find that it isn't him.

The sound of the bell chimes as the door swings open. With her back turned to me, Clara begins stumbling into the store, dragging a large piece of plywood through the entrance. I race to help her, grabbing the door and propping it open as she pulls the wood along the floor, dropping it in front of the window nook.

"Did he show yet?" she asks, wiping her sawdust covered palms against the front of her jeans. I swallow, shaking my head solemnly.

"No."

She walks over to me, and nudges my side with her elbow. "Perk up, bud. He's probably on his way right now."

I want to tell her about the sinking feeling forming in my chest. I want to express how uncomfortable the twisting of my gut is. How, for some inexplicable reason, I have this thought building inside of me. One that Marcus might not show after all.

But Clara has had enough of my "woe is me" shit throughout the years. I know how exhausting I can be, always complaining about the glass half empty, just to suck more water out of it. It's not time to turn this into one of those episodes. Not yet, at least.

"I can get the rest of it," I offer, forcing a feigned smile to stretch across my lips. Clara's expression brightens, and she pats my back enthusiastically.

"That's it!" she exclaims. "He'll be here in no time."

5:00PM

Crimson is my favorite color, so it's no mystery why I always run toward red flags rather than away from them. Maybe Marcus was right.

Maybe I *am* addicted to being sad, and this was some sick form of self-sabotage. God, why did I do this to myself?

The switch clicks in Clara's palm, the glow of the "open" sign flicking to abrupt lightless, void of color.

"Maybe he has a late flight?" she offers optimistically. I shake my head, letting it fall into my hands as my elbows rest atop the desk.

"The last one left at 3:30. I checked," I answer. I'd expect some sort of whine to tug at my voice, something that shows how badly my heart is breaking. But maybe that's just it. I'm already so broken, there's nothing else that could really and truly ruin me. Perhaps it's for the better, because if I were able to feel the depths of this, I don't think I would make it out alive.

Clara's head hangs, and she approaches me, plopping onto the desk, and slowly rocking my swiveling chair back and forth with her foot. She doesn't say anything, and I appreciate it. Because there really is nothing to say. I fell for it. *Again.* I allowed myself to believe, for some stupid fleeting moment, that someone could see me in my entirety, all the pain, all the sadness, all the annoying wallowing, and still care enough to love me. I should know better than that by now, but I guess in the end, everyone craves unquestioning love. Maybe it's just not for me.

"No," Clara cuts in firmly. "No, I'm not going to let you do that."

My head lifts from my hands, and I look at her, numbness washing over me.

"Do what?"

She gestures to my face, her palm sticking out toward my nose and moving in circles.

"*That.* The *'I'm unlovable'* thing that runs your self-destructive brain. I'm not letting it happen, Kane."

My brows weave together, and a sharp scoff slips from my lips. "Clara, I—"

"No." She shakes her head. "Just, *no*, Kane. I know you can't always control it. I know it's always there, sitting in the back of your mind, but you need to stop giving it so much credibility. Do you firmly believe every thought that enters your brain?"

I swallow, a dry ache settling into the center of my throat. "No," I admit. "But—"

"But *nothing*, Kane. What do you think I'm still here for, charity?" She scoffs, crossing her arms annoyedly over her chest. "If I wanted to perform charity, I'd volunteer at the soup kitchen."

"You do," I mumble, and she lightly bops the side of my head.

"Nope! It's *my* turn. So just-" She huffs. "Just shut up and listen. If Derrick and I didn't want to be there through your ups and downs, we wouldn't be. If I didn't want to hang around you, I'd give you my half of the store and go spend my days with Judah at the beach. I know you're lonely, Kane. And I know you will never stop loving Marcus. But don't let his dickwad behavior prevent you from seeing the love you already have."

Tears begin to well in my eyes as Clara speaks. I try to take a steadying breath, but no words come from my lips, so she continues.

"Derrick never shuts up about you. Dickie *pees* every time you walk in the door. God! Do you know how shitty it feels to rip your vagina open just to birth a baby that loves your ex-husband more than he loves you? You have more love in your life than there are stars in the goddamned sky."

Tears stream down my face now, my cheeks growing wet and raw as the salt rubs against them. I don't know how I got so lucky with Clara, but I'll spend the rest of my life trying to deserve it. She uses the soft pad of her thumb to wipe the tears away, but the river continues, and she pulls me close instead.

"You are *lovable*," she whispers, running her hand through my hair. "And I don't expect you to always remember it. But you have to at least try to believe me when I'm sitting here, telling you. Okay?"

A heavy pulse thrums in my temples as I listen to her words. They sink into my skin, embedding themselves into my stomach and chest like shrapnel. It stings, and burns, and a soft sob slips through my lips at the sensation. But although it hurts, something about it feels peaceful too. Like it's all been coated with cold aloe, soothing the pain. I don't have a partner or a spouse. I lost the one person I've ever truly been in love with, *twice*. But Clara is right. That doesn't negate the other relationships I've built. It doesn't make the love I share with her, and Judah, and Derrick, and even Dickie, worth less. I sniff, an unpleasant stuffy sound coming from my nose as I nod, my lip trembling.

"Okay," I reply, aggressively wiping the tears on my cheeks. There's a slight burn to it, the skin swollen and sensitive. Clara hands me a tissue, and the sound of an elephant pierces the air as I blow into it. Silence follows, but when our eyes lock together, we both burst into a teary fit of bittersweet laughter.

"You wanna kick some shit?" she asks, her brow lifted to display her intrigue. I ponder it for a moment. Really, I'm just exhausted. I want to crawl in bed, and sleep for seventeen hours. But as Clara looks at me, with full love and care and intent to make me feel better, I know I should stay. Even if it's more for her than it is for me.

That's another thing I've learned throughout the years. Those who don't understand it will tell you that everything you do must be for yourself. There's a myth, that if you don't love yourself, nobody else will either. You have to get out of bed, eat, drink water, and be productive, for *you*. Because how can someone love somebody who hates themselves?

The same way an author can despise their own book, while thousands of readers cherish it. How an artist's least favorite painting can sell for millions. How musicians get sick of singing the same song, over and over, but listeners around the world play it on loop because they just can't get enough.

It's easy to dislike something when you can't escape it. But that doesn't mean it's worthless. It doesn't mean authors shouldn't continue to write, or musicians shouldn't continue to play. And it definitely doesn't mean that you shouldn't continue to live.

"Yeah," I nod. "Yeah, I think I do."

After Clara clears the new wood away from the nook bench, and relocates Dickie's bed to the cubby below the desk, I pull my leg back, twist my ankle slightly, and deliver the first blow.

The plywood cracks, a small piece of it caving inside of the structure. I hate to admit that for some strange reason, it does make me feel better. I flash Clara a grin, stepping to the side to allow her to take a turn.

"I'm pretending it's you, by the way," she says, making full eye contact with me as her foot glides through the aged wood. My hands toss up defensively, and I take a weary step back.

"Why me?"

She struggles to pry her foot from the jagged hole it's created, so her hands settle along the top of it to create leverage.

"Because—" she grunts, tugging back with full force until her foot breaks free. "I grew a baby in my stomach for nine months and he likes you more than me."

A slight smile tugs at the corner of my mouth, and I try really hard to hide it, but from the furrow of Clara's brow, I can say confidently that I have failed.

"Oh, you meant that?" I ask, pulling my leg back again. This time, I position the bottom of my heel outward as I deliver the blow. The wood crashes, tumbling to the floor, and scattering about a splintered mess. A soft chuckle escapes my lips, and I pat her gently on the shoulder. "Come on, Clara. He loves you."

She shoots me an expression that I'm sure should concern me, and motions for me to step back. I comply, feeling my eyes widen as she picks up a crowbar, gripping it tightly in her hands.

"Yeah, yeah." She shoves the sloped end of it beneath the top piece of wood and the frame, using her weight to wedge it in as far as it can go. "Do you want to do the honors, or should I?"

Exhaustion fills my bones, and as much as I'd like to give Clara the show I know she wants, I don't think I could pry that piece of wood up if I tried.

"All yours," I say, drawing up my arm and flexing my bicep. "Show me those mom muscles."

A bright grin stretches across Clara's face, and she gives the crowbar one last shove before leaning down, and pressing all her weight against it.

The eroded board lets out a high-pitched creaking sound, little snapping fibers of wood surrounding it as Clara puts all her muscle behind the movement. It begins to lift, bending and snapping at the corners until finally, it breaks free. Clara howls, jumping up and waving the crowbar around like it doesn't possess the ability to severely injure someone.

"Clara," I say warningly. "Put the crowbar down."

Her eyes roll, but she listens, gently lowering it to the floor, then pulling the large piece of wood off the top, and tossing it to the side. Her body leans over the frame of the nook, her nose wrinkling as she peers at it.

"Ew," she says, her mouth contorting into a very disgusted frown. "It's *really* dusty." She leans in closer, her forehead now following her nose in a wrinkling motion.

"What?" I ask. She shrugs, reaching her hand down into the frame.

"I don't know," she answers, fishing for something inside. "It's—"

Her hand pulls out, and wedged between her dust-stained fingers, is a small, folded piece of paper, a dust bunny clinging to the corner of it. She carefully pulls the ball of dust off, dropping it carelessly onto the floor.

"Do you think it's a treasure map?" she asks excitedly. I chuckle, stepping closer to her to get a better look.

"I've been working here for twenty-four years, Clara. If there was hidden treasure somewhere inside this place, I think I would've found it by now."

Her fingers dip between the worn folds of the paper, and she begins carefully pulling the corners open. I slide even closer, pressing the side of my body against hers, as she unfolds every crease in the note, stretching it out for us both to see. But just as my eyes begin to focus on the paper, Clara's hand begins shaking, and the ink scrawled across the page grows blurry.

"Kane—" Her voice breaks, and she turns to look at me, pressing the note into my chest. I take the page from her trembling fingers, and hold it out in front of me. When my eyes land on it, I no longer notice the folds or the dust. The only thing I can focus on is the handwriting. Scripted and dark, smudged ink stained across the sides is a familiarity

I have never forgotten. My graze draws up to the top of the page, and I begin to read it.

Kane,

I don't have much time, so I hope the lack of creativity and poetry in this letter doesn't disappoint you. Here's the deal:

My parents have found out about us. I know I've spent this entire summer trying to hide it from them, but I have to admit, it feels good that they know. They weren't kind, or understanding, nor did I expect them to be. But I realized, as they were screaming and tossing my things about the house, that I don't give a flying fuck about their opinions anymore.

God, I'm late. I know I am, and I couldn't be more sorry.

I've spent half of our time together, pushing you away. Denying how I felt, because I was scared of them. I realize now, how stupid it was, because the only thing I should have ever been scared of was losing you. If they get to you before you find this, don't believe anything they say, for the thing I am most grateful for in this life has always been you. Because of you, I know who I am.

I might be too late. I might have pushed you away enough to make you hate me. But if it isn't, and if I haven't, meet me at the train station by 3PM tomorrow. When we start our new life, I will scream my love for you from the rooftops, and not give a fuck who hears it.   -MF

I read the note, again and again. I don't know if I'm hoping that the words transition into something new, or if I'm begging for the thought that what is in front of me, is truly reality. Heat expands inside of my stomach, and my vision grows fuzzy as tears crate a thick coat of gloss over my eyes. Clara places her arm around my shoulders, squeezing them gently.

"He— He left a note," I manage to say, my voice cracking. Clara's head tips into my shoulder as she continues to hug me.

"It appears so," she answers softly. My body shakes, my chest moving up and down vigorously as I try to catch my crying breath.

"All this time, I thought—" I hiccup, tears pooling in the corners of my mouth, bringing a salty taste to my lips. "I thought he just left. I thought—"

"You thought he abandoned you."

I nod, swallowing back the ache forming in my throat. The sore muscles tense as I try to hold in my cries, but they break under the pressure, releasing it all. Clara keeps holding me, using her hand to brush away the hair sticking to my tear-stained cheeks. Her body shakes alongside mine as I take staggered, airy breaths. For twenty years, I've resented Marcus. For abandoning me, for denying me, to his parents and himself. And this entire time, Marcus had waited for me. He planned for me to come with him.

"Kane," she whispers, her breath warm against my cheek. I don't try to fight the tears anymore. I just look over at her, my eyes stinging from the salty glaze. She swipes a falling tear, a soft smile tugging at her lips. "Do you know what this means?"

My brows pinch together, and I sniff, confused. "What?"

The pressure around my body releases as she pulls away from me, looking up into my eyes with an electric glow. I only grow more confused.

"Kane," she repeats, like I need a preparation. I take a deep breath, ready to hear her take. "He probably left you one this time too."

My stomach sinks, and I immediately shake my head. "No," I answer, matter-of-factly. "There's no way Marcus could have left a note in here. I was here until seven last night, and the doors were locked until I opened this morning."

I appreciate Clara's optimism. She's always the first person in the room to jump to a happy conclusion, and it's a nice change from my more dreary point of view. But Marcus leaving behind a second note? Well, it's just not possible.

However, my point doesn't seem to have gotten across to Clara, because that bright smile still conquers her face. I take a deep breath, preparing myself to explain, again, why Marcus could not have left a note. Why, in fact, he's probably a thousand miles away, hating me for never showing up to that train station. But light flickers in her eyes, she rushes to the back room, Dickie chasing behind her.

I quickly follow, the worn soles of my sandals slapping against the hardwood. I don't know what's gotten into her, but she needs to do what I've already done: Accept it. Accept the fact that Marcus is gone, and I blew my chance at being with him twenty years ago. When I reach the doorway, I linger in it for a moment. Clara's eyes are wide and wild, and papers are sprawled all across her desk. On top of them, an open laptop.

"We have to get into the email," she insists, her fingers dancing crazily across the keyboard. I cock my head, staring at the mess in front of me.

"Why?"

She pulls her cell phone from her pocket, dialing a set of numbers before pressing it to her ear. "Because." She takes a deep breath, then flashes me a beaming smile. "I think he left you a note after all."

Chapter Eighteen

MARCUS

"Thank you so much for coming." I force a smile as I draw my repetitive black signature across the title page, for what feels like the thousandth time today. "Your support means the world to me."

I feel my stomach twist as I speak the sentence, which has also, likely, been said about a thousand times today. It's not like I'm lying. I could never accurately express how grateful I am for my readers, because without them, I might not have ever felt comfortable being myself. It's just hard to sit here with a grin plastered across my face, when I still haven't heard from Kane.

I shouldn't have left. I should have just sent Nellie back here, and had her hand out pre-signed copies. But she was right. Her name would have been attached to that decision too, and I make her life hard enough as it is. It's shocking how I can write five-hundred pages of pure, literary genius, and not think to ask Kane for his phone number. I had planned to, yesterday morning before I left, but I should have done it the night before, when he was rushing out the door to go meet Clara. I should have fought for him to stay a moment longer, just like I should have fought for him twenty years ago.

But I ruined it all. And now, he'll likely do whatever he can to forget me.

"We're past time," Janelle whispers, flashing me her phone screen. I glance up at her, then to the long line of anxious readers, excitedly awaiting their turn. "Should I tell them to go home?"

"No." I shake my head, then smile and wave for the next person to step up. "They've been waiting hours."

Janelle nods understandingly, then places a few new hardcovers onto the table beside me. Two elderly men step up to the table, both boasting beaming grins.

"Hello, Carsen," one says in a hoarse yet mousy voice. Something I love about my readers is that they're so diverse. There isn't one particular group of people who read my books. They're for everyone, from age eighteen to ninety-four. Seriously, I had a ninety-four year old woman approach me at a convention. But I guess that's the beautiful thing about art. It's for everyone.

"Hi!" I smile, and strangely, this one comes with ease. It may be the first smile today that I didn't have to beg to appear. "What are your names?"

The taller man's cheeks grow a deep shade of red, while the shorter one answers for him. "He's James, and I'm Frederick."

I look to James, allowing our eyes to lock before I say: "It's very nice to meet you."

An even wider smile breaks across his face, showing off his worn dentures. "Likewise," he says, his tone flustered and sweet. "I'm a really big fan. Well, we both are."

"Yeah?" I slide one of the copies in front of me, flipping open the cover to personalize it. "Which is your favorite?"

James looks even more nervous now, glancing at Frederick as if seeking the confidence to speak. It's sweet that even at this age, they are there for each other. He takes a slow breath, looking back to me.

"Well, Freddy likes *The Jones Diary*." He chuckles, the color in his cheeks deepening. I didn't take Freddy for a freak, but for some reason, it makes me proud. "And me? Well, I've always loved the original, *Harrison's Affair*."

Something in my stomach begins to sink, or, flutter, maybe? Nobody's favorite is ever *Harrison's Affair*. Nobody but Kane, of course. There are so many mistakes in that book, so many things I could've done better. But even to this day, it's not something I'd ever change. I wrote that story the way I needed to at the time. It's such a personal part of me, I hadn't ever really considered that others would love it the way I do. I begin to scrawl out the men's names on their books, following it with my signature.

"Why *Harrison's Affair?*" I ask curiously. My heart begins to thump in my chest, and I swear I get a whiff of coconut from one of the men. It reminds me of kissing Kane in the lighthouse, the way his cologne smells and how his lips tasted. Not just that night, but before. When we'd walk to Sully's then hide for hours in Roberta's, kissing and talking and touching. It makes me think of the years in between, when we could have been doing just that. I should have waited. I shouldn't have just left some dumb note for him to find, and think it was enough for him to follow me. After the months of hiding, the back and forth of it all, I don't see how it could be. Kane deserved more than a letter. Hell, he deserved more than a book. He deserved what James and Frederick have: A lifetime of love.

James' hands begin to shake, and he settles his weight onto the cane gripped in his hand. "*Harrison's Affair* is what made me realize I was gay."

"What?" My lungs deflate as the words echo off the inside of my skull. "Wait, so how long have you guys been together?"

James and Frederick exchange a bashful glance, then look back to me proudly. "Four years," Frederick answers. "Actually, we met at book club." He grins. "*Harrison's Affair.*"

James nods affirmingly. "Best four years of my life."

Heat swells in my chest, and instead of smiling at the couple in front of me, I stare down at the page my hand is rested on so that tears don't have the opportunity to well in my eyes. Simeon is already going to be pissed off enough when he finds out that I'm quitting traditional publishing. The last thing I need is for him to hear about how I bawled my eyes out in the middle of a signing. I allow the cold air to crystalize my eyes, before clearing my throat, and smiling up at them.

Here are two people who, even with the short time they have left, found one another and did not let go. Two people who spent a lifetime apart, and still spent their happiest years together. *Hell,* if James and Frederick aren't too late, then maybe Kane and I aren't either.

"It was really nice to meet you two," I say, sliding their books over to them. "Really, you guys are beautiful."

The couple nods sweetly at me, and Frederick carries the books as James slowly begins to walk away. I quickly look up at Janelle with desperate eyes.

"Book me the first ticket to Portland," I say, the thrumming in my chest growing louder. "Please."

Janelle nods, glancing up at the crowd in front of us. She leans in, her temple pressing against mine, and lowers her voice to a whisper.

"I don't think I have to," she says, gesturing to the crowd. My brows drop, and I'm about to tell her to "just book the damn thing" when I look to the next person standing in line.

"Do you mind?" Kane asks, raising his brows as he sets a book in front of me. I stare at him, blinking slowly as if his face will change into a stranger's if I look long enough. A soft chuckle slips from his lips, and he steps even closer to me, the familiar scent of coconut now fully conquering my senses. I want to grab him, plant my lips onto his, and turn this entire bookstore into the background of our happily ever after. Instead, I point at him, then to the book, then back at him, as if that conveys any articulate message of love or longing.

"You—" I stutter, tilting my head with confusion. "But—" I stop again. It seems that my aptitude for words has simply ceased in Kane's presence, because every time my lips part to speak, nothing more than a word seems to tumble out. I don't understand. I left him, again, with nothing more than a note. One he didn't even respond to. How is he here right now? Why do I have the privilege of staring at the beautiful mess in front of me? Of smelling his scent, and feeling his gaze?

"What?" Kane asks, and I swear his voice is almost taunting. "Don't have the words, for once?" He pushes the book across the table to me, and I glance down at it, the foiled title flashing at me like a neon sign. "I figured I may as well add it to my collection. Books are worth a lot more if they're signed, y'know."

There's no fighting it now, and Simeon is going to be pissed. Tears well in my eyes and I stand up shakily. Kane doesn't hesitate any longer. He hurdles himself around the edge of my table, throwing his arms around me and pulling me in so tight that I can't breathe. But if this were the way I go out, I'd gladly die a thousand deaths. His body wraps around mine like a boa constrictor, my nose pressed into his broad shoulders as tears stream down my face.

"I got your letter," he whispers, his hand stroking the back of my neck. My knees shake beneath my weight, and I take a shuddered breath, gripping the back of his shirt tightly.

"Why didn't you respond?" I ask, my voice breaking. Kane's embrace releases, his fingers drawing to his back pocket to retrieve something.

"Not your email," he explains. "Though I got those eventually too." He holds up a small folded piece of paper, years of dust staining the outside of it. "This note. The one you left the first time. Clara found it under the window nook. I didn't—" His voice cracks, but he continues to speak. "I would have come. If I knew, Marcus, I would have come."

My pulse quickens, my throat tightening as Kane brings me back to that day. All this time, I thought he didn't come because of how I treated our relationship. Like it was a casual fling, like we were never really going to be together. Because it took being outed to my parents to accept myself, I thought that Kane had simply grown tired of it all. And I accepted it so easily, because it was *fair*. I denied our relationship to anyone who asked. I made him hide in a goddamned lighthouse with me, because I didn't want us to be seen together too often.

I sat at that train station for four hours, waiting for Kane. And the entire time, he didn't even know it.

"You're here now," I say, tracing his cheek with my palm. Tears prick Kane's eyes, and his hand wraps around the small of my back, pulling me close to him.

"I love you, Marcus. I have loved you for twenty years, and you make me want to be around for twenty more, just so that I can keep loving you." He tilts his chin up, grips the back of my neck, and presses our lips together. Sunlight beams through my body, filling up my chest as Kane's lips dance tenderly with mine. How I went twenty years without this, I could never say. All I know is that right here, right now, marks the moment when our life really begins.

One Year Later

"Are you ready, my love?" I call through the door. A loud huff billows through the wood, followed by a series of frustrated stomps. The lock clicks, then, hesitantly, the door swings open.

"It doesn't fit anymore!" Kane groans, his head falling to his hands. I look at him, head tilted as I analyze his tightly-fitting tux. The button holes are stretched, the black fabric appearing somewhat translucent against the white dress shirt below it. I smile, cradling his chin in my hand and lifting it up so that he has no choice but to look at me. His thick brows are furrowed over his narrowed eyes, and he lets out another displeased sound. "It's the stupid Zoloft," he grumbles. "I look like shit."

I lean forward, placing my lips gently against the crown of his head. "Don't talk about my soon-to-be husband that way," I say, brushing a strand of hair from his face. "You look ridiculously handsome."

Nellie pops into the bedroom. She looks stunning, as always. The dark green jumpsuit she's wearing compliments her eyes, and her hair is pulled up into gorgeous, shiny Zulu knots.

"Are you ready to go?" she asks, her French-tipped nails tapping impatiently against her thigh. "We were supposed to be there twenty minutes ago. I didn't push my publishing date so that you could miss your own wedding."

Kane's brows furrow, and he shoots her a confused glance. "You pushed your publishing date because your editor is getting married." He gestures to himself.

"We'll be there in a minute, " I say, and she nods, stepping back and pulling the door closed behind her. I turn back to Kane, unbuttoning his suit jacket. "You don't need this." I toss it carelessly onto the bed, like it were a candy wrapper or an old receipt, rather than a thousand dollar jacket. "I don't care about what you wear to our wedding, Kane. I don't care if your new medication has made you gain weight, or if you can't get out of bed tomorrow because you're so exhausted, or if you get so trashed at the reception that I have to carry you home. All I care about is that when we're standing at the end of the isle, you say 'I do' and mean it." Kane sighs, and I find his hand, squeezing it. "Is that still what you want?"

His chin tilts up to look at me, and he nods. "Yes."

A smile breaks across my face, and I reach for his bow tie, straightening it out. "Then let's go see Roberta."

"Do you think it's weird to have our wedding in a haunted lighthouse?" he asks, following me to the door.

I shake my head. "No. I think it's romantic." I kiss the side of his temple as I open the door, allowing him to step through it first. "Like the rest of our love story."

"Yeah," he smiles, entangling his fingers with mine. "It was pretty well written."

i pretend there will be a day,
where sirens turn to wedding
bells,
the breeze to rose petals,
my even-toned finger to a band
of sunless white
and these letters to vows
for you to be forever mine

-MF

Caution

The following epilogue contains material that some may deem disqualifying of the romance genre. If you are sensitive to death, or do not wish to subjectively turn this romance into a love story, please leave the story as it is, and do not continue further. Know, however, that in my eyes, given the themes of the book, that this is, in fact, a happily ever after.

Epilogue

KANE

Forty-Three Years Later

Waves crash against the shore like a song, the sound funneling through the open window of my kitchen. So much salt fills the air that I can taste it, the familiar flavor of the ocean breeze after a storm. I lean forward in my chair, closing one of Marcus' old novels and setting it onto the coffee table. My eyes drift over to him, the forest green urn staring back at me.

"He looks good next to Dickie," Clara says, shakily gripping her cup of tea. Judah grabs her hand, carefully steadying it as she takes a sip. Even though Clara has aged, her skin wrinkled and hair cut into a grey and white bob, they bear so much resemblance. He looks exactly like her, actually. Blonde hair and eyes so green you'd swear they're gemstones. Except his nose. That, he got from Derrick.

"He does."

"Daddy, can we go play in the play room?" a small voice asks. Judah looks to his children, Isla and Imogen, adjusting the green sound processor hooked around his ear.

"You'll have to ask Grunkle Kane. It's his room, after all."

I roll my eyes, waving off the girls to go play with their Barbies and Godzilla action figures. "Oh quiet, Judah. You know that room is more theirs than it is mine."

Judah smiles, helping Clara set her tea down onto the table.

"They should still ask," he says. "They're like little twin tornados every time they go into a room."

"So were you," I reply coyly, and Clara lets out a loud laugh.

"It's true," she says. "I think you might have been worse."

Judah laughs, shaking his head. "You just say that because I was your child, and they're your grandkids."

Clara twirls a finger in the air like an invisible siren. "Bingo."

A tired chuckle slips through my lips, and I lean back into my chair, sighing.

"Before I forget," Judah says, pulling himself up from the couch. "I have something for you. I found it in the back room at the store."

My brows raise interrogatorily. "Are you taking care of her?"

Clara leans across the table to lightly smack me. "Oh, shush Kane. You know Judah loves that place just as much as you."

Judah nods, and I release my accusatory glare, raising my hands up in acceptance. "Alright, alright. Just making sure."

"I just have to run out to the car. I'll be back," he says. When he closes the front door behind him, Clara leans in closer to me, now boasting her own skeptical stare. I frown.

"What, Claire?"

She shrugs. "I just want to check in on you. After Derrick passed, well..." She sighs softly. "I just am worried about you."

"You should worry about that grandkid of yours who keeps shoving crayons up her nose," I grunt. Clara laughs, the wrinkles around her nose deepening.

"Why does she keep doing that? Judah never did."

I tilt my head, squinting my eyes as if I'm trying to see a distant memory. "Didn't you?"

Clara's brows weave together in confusion. "What?"

"I swear I remember you getting a lollipop stuck up your nose in the first grade."

Clara pauses for a moment, letting her eyes wander to the ceiling as she tries to recall the memory.

"You know, I think I did."

"Here it is," Judah announces, plopping back onto the couch. He sets something onto the coffee table, a faded light blue book. I stare at it, confused as to why there are empty spots on the cover and spine, where the title should be. I continue to analyze it, knowing that for some reason, this book is familiar. And the moment my fingertips rub against it, I immediately realize why.

"Where did you get this?" I ask, my voice weak and shaky.

"The back room," he responds. "I've never seen it before, but it just appeared there, in the desk drawer. I didn't know what it was, so I opened it, and— Well, I figured you should have it."

I reach out, placing my weathered hand onto Judah's and squeezing it softly. "Thank you," I whisper. "Thank you for finding it."

"We'll be back Sunday, Sugar Kane!" Clara calls out, stumbling over the loose tennis ball that popped off her walker. Judah catches her, helping her into the car before waving goodbye to me.

"Love you, Uncle Kane!" He smiles. "Call me if you need anything!"

I nod, watching as the car pulls out of the driveway, and disappears down the road. When they are no longer in sight, I close the front door, hobbling over to my chair. The wood creaks, the seat rocking as my weight piles against it when I sit down. I reach out for the novel I had been reading earlier, but my eye catches onto that blue faux book. It's worn, just like me. Small scuffs settled into the cloth, indents pressed into the hardcover. I pick it up, set it onto my lap, and take a shuddered breath as I open it.

Just like I remember, it's filled with letters. Little, ink-smudged notes from decades ago, still bearing the same love I've felt all these years. I remember the last one I put in here: the lost gesture that brought us back together. Marcus continued to write me letters, only, I couldn't find the box. So I hung them on the fridge, and placed them in picture frames, and stapled them together like my own personal collection of sonnets. But I missed this box, and the letters inside.

As my aged fingers dig through the notes, my eye catches on one that stands out from the rest. There is no dust, or ink smudges. The creases appear crisp, and new. And the paper... Well, it's exactly like the stationary Marcus used until his passing last month. Beige and blue watercolor, a thick and textured feel. I pick it up, pressing my glasses up the bridge of my nose to get a better look at it.

My Handsome Kane,

If you're reading this, well, I am no longer here. The cancer has grown terminal, and I'm sorry you had to find out about it the way you did. If I had told you, I knew you'd spend your days worrying about me, instead of just being with me. I always thought I'd be the one to bury you. It was a fear of mine, actually. Something I spent years trying to cope with, because I never knew if one day, you would just leave. It's a privilege to write this note, because it means I gave you enough reason to stay. I am so proud of you, handsome. For how loving you are, how forgiving, and how strong. The life I had was long, but with you, never long enough. Thank you for helping me love myself. I hope, in some way, I accomplished the same for you. Know that even though I am not here, my love for you is as alive as it was the day I met you. Goodbye, my love. I'll give Dickie a kiss for you. -MF

Tears well in my eyes, and I shakily press the note to my chest, looking over at Marcus. I didn't think that I'd ever make it to this age, much less outlive him. He always had so much life in him, even during his last days. But despite the fact that it's never been easy for me, and regardless of how much I miss Marcus, I'm grateful I stayed until the end. Because I got to do it with him.

About the Author

Elle Sprinkle is a contemporary romance author known for her narratives centered around marginalized communities, including the LGBT community, disabled individuals, and those living with chronic illnesses. Originally from Rockport, Texas, Elle now resides in Idaho, where she continues to cultivate heartfelt, smutty stories.

Before her official debut in 2024 with the novel "Puppy Love," Elle had been a lifelong writer. Being raised with deep evangelical roots, writing became a form of self expression that she previously had no safe channel for. From short stories to poetry, coping with internalized homophobia and mental illness slowly became easier. Today, when she's not weaving romantic tales, Elle can be found binge-watching true crime series, snuggling with her five beloved dogs, or paddle boarding with her stunning wife.

Printed in Dunstable, United Kingdom

63870608R00117